365
Moral
Stories

All religions have the
same morals
that shape humans.

Om
K*DZ Om Books International

Reprinted in 2021

Corporate & Editorial Office
A-12, Sector 64, Noida 201 301
Uttar Pradesh, India
Phone: +91 120 477 4100
Email: editorial@ombooks.com
Website: www.ombooksinternational.com

Sales Office
107, Ansari Road, Darya Ganj
New Delhi 110 002, India
Phone: +91 11 4000 9000
Email: sales@ombooks.com

© Om Books International 2015

ISBN: 978-93-84225-31-5

Printed in India

10 9 8 7 6 5

365 Moral Stories

All religions have the same morals that shape humans.

Om
KIDZ
An imprint of Om Books International

Contents

March

April

July

October

November

1 The Short-tempered Demon

Once upon a time, there was a very short-tempered demon. He would get angry at the smallest things. When angry, he had no control over his actions.

One day, the demon decided to make for himself a beautiful tree house for the summer. He worked hard for ten days. On the eleventh day, a beautiful tree house was ready on the tallest tree of the jungle. Just when the demon was giving it the final touches, a pigeon flying above him dropped a worm on his shoulder.

The demon was furious and started chasing the pigeon. After a long chase the tired pigeon sat on top of a tree. The demon was so blinded by rage that he didn't realise that it was the same tree with his precious tree house. He lashed out at it and his beautiful tree house came crashing down along with the tree.

Thoughtless anger can cause serious damage.

② Suzy's Ice cream Party

There was a girl named Suzy. One day, she decided to call her friends for an ice cream party. She mixed the ingredients and kept them in the freezer to set.

After a few minutes, Suzy grew very impatient. She opened the freezer to see if the ice cream was ready. It wasn't. Every ten minutes, she checked the fridge. The freezer got warmer every time it was opened. Even after four hours, the ice cream failed to set. To make matters worse, just when Suzy's friends were about to arrive, the fridge broke down.

Suzy's ice cream party was ruined.

Impatience is the mother of mistakes.

③ Fingers and the Thumb

Once, all the fingers of the hand ganged up against the thumb. The shapely fingers teased the thumb for being short and stout.

They teased him, "Ugly Thumb! Ugly Thumb!"

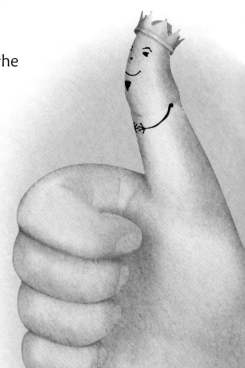

The thumb grew sad and decided not to be in the company of the fingers anymore. He sat there, unmoving. When the hand needed to write or hold anything, it couldn't. The fingers realised that even though the thumb didn't look like them, he was more useful than all of them.

The fingers apologised to the thumb and the hand began working again!

Utility is more important than beauty.

4 Blue Patch in the Sky

Tim and his Grandma planned to spend one whole day at the beach. When Tim began packing his picnic bag, he saw big, dark clouds gathering in the sky.

"Oh, no!" Tim exclaimed. The clouds thundered and soon it began to rain havily.

"Please, Grandma," Tim pleaded. "Let's not cancel our trip."

"Don't worry, Tim," Grandma said. "We will definitely go if we see a bright blue patch in the sky."

Tim sat by the window and waited for the blue patch to appear. The rain stopped, but the clouds refused to part. Then Tim had an idea. He decided to enjoy on his own till the clouds parted. He ran to his room and fetched a blue handkerchief from the cupboard. He went to the terrace and started waving his blue handkerchief, pretending that it was the blue sky. He clapped and laughed and called out to the birds on trees.

Grandma, who was glancing at her wet plants in the garden, looked up just then and smiled.

"The clouds have indeed parted," she said. And they had! It seemed that looking at little Tim's efforts, the Sun had smiled and peeped out from behind the clouds. This created a bright blue patch in the sky, just above the handkerchief that Tim was waving!

Make the most of an unpleasant situation.

5 The Elephant and the Ant

One day, an elephant and an ant went for a walk to the mountain top. The elephant was boasting about his weight. He said to the ant, "If I were to fall on you, you would die."

Suddenly, the Earth shook and the ground beneath them gave away. Both of them fell off the mountain. The elephant fell hard and fractured his leg, but the ant gracefully floated down to where the elephant lay groaning.

"I think I am happy being so light," the ant said and called a doctor for the elephant.

Bigger is not always better.

6 Sluggy Learns a Lesson

Sluggy was a young snail. Once he was tired of carrying his shell on his back. He threw it away and began prancing around without his shell. Soon, he came across a wise old snail.

The old snail asked Sluggy, "Why aren't you carrying your shell with you? It is also your house."

"Why should I?" Sluggy answered.

"We carry our houses so that we have a place to take shelter whenever it rains," the old snail answered. After some time, it started raining. The old snail comfortably retreated into his shell and remained warm, while Sluggy got all drenched and squishy.

Be prepared for the rainy day.

7 Tina and the Giant

Tina always wondered what was in the dark forest that lay behind her house. Everyone had warned her not to go there.

"There lives a big, bad giant out there," warned her aunt.

One day, when her parents were visiting a friend in the neighbouring town, Tina decided to explore the big, bad forest herself. She strolled in, lightly whistling as she walked on the dry grass.

She was deep inside the forest when she saw a giant, who was ten times her size. He stood right in front of her.

"Mmmmm, here comes my dinner," he said and laughed in an evil manner.

"Oh no! Look, another giant!" Tina shrieked and pointed behind him. Just as the giant turned around, Tina ran. She ran all the way to her house and locked the door.

The giant couldn't run as fast as her because he was too big and heavy. Tina's presence of mind had saved her.

After that day, Tina swore never to go into the dark forest again.

Quick thinking can help you in any situation.

8 The Pigeon's Nest

On a lazy Sunday afternoon, George and his friends saw a pigeon taking one twig at a time from the barn. The boys started observing the pigeon. They wondered what he was doing. The pigeon flew from the barn to the tree and back again.

   At the end of the day, the pigeon had a beautiful nest ready on the tree. He had managed to make an entire nest by taking one twig at a time. As the sun set far away on the horizon, the pigeon peacefully slept in his nest.

The journey of a thousand miles begins with a single step.

9 June and the Cupcakes

Once there was a very greedy girl named June. Her friend Alice invited her to a birthday party. At the party, there were lots of cupcakes kept on the table. June, being the greedy girl that she was, wanted to gobble up all the cupcakes. She began eating them. First she ate one, then two, and finally she finished twenty cupcakes!

The next morning, June woke up with a stomachache. She could barely move. That day, the entire class went for a picnic. June lay in bed, groaning with pain. She swore that she would stop being so greedy.

Greed gets you nothing.

10 Julia Feeds Her Fish

Once there was a little girl named Julia. On her eighth birthday, her friend gifted her a tiny, orange fish in a plastic bag filled with water. Julia was thrilled. She named it Fishy. Julia brought a fish bowl and put Fishy in it. She walked down to the pet shop and bought a tiny box of fish food. It said, "Feed one teaspoon at a time, no more".

On the first day, Julia did what was instructed on the box. But Fishy kept opening its mouth continuously. On the second day, Julia decided to give it a little more. Little by little, she fed Fishy the whole box within an hour.

Poor fishy overate and soon it died.

Julia lost her cute little friend. She felt bad at not following the instructions.

Indulgence is as bad as deprivation.

11 Joe's Laughter

There was once a boy named Joe. He laughed at everyone's problems. If a friend fell into a ditch, Joe would laugh. If his mother happened to burn the pudding, he would laugh. Sadly, Joe never helped anyone. He paid no attention to his mother's advice on being compassionate like his sister Nancy, who helped anyone in need and never laughed at others' problems.

One day, Joe and Nancy were going to school. It was raining and the road was filled with muddy puddles. Suddenly, a car sped by and splashed their uniform with mud. Joe's friends started laughing. They laughed and laughed, but no one came forward to help him. Nancy's friends rushed to help her clean her uniform.

What goes around comes around.

12 Jill's Great Day

There was once a girl named Jill who was very happy since it was her birthday. She loved the way her friends and teachers were fussing over her. Jill was so busy enjoying her perfect day that she didn't notice that her best friend, Paula, was in pain. Poor Paula was having a toothache.

Jill, not caring about Paula's plight, offered her a chocolate cookie. Gasp!

A cookie during a toothache is a really bad idea. Paula got angry with Jill and decided never to talk to her again. Jill lost a friend because she was too busy thinking about herself.

A friend who does not understand is not a friend at all.

13 The Class Test

On a bright Monday morning, Madam Elephant declared that she would hold a very difficult test the following week. She also said that the one who scored the least would be punished. The class shuddered at this declaration. Tortoise, Crocodile and Monkey started planning the way they would study for the test. Hare just sat in one corner, lazily munching on a carrot. As usual, he was overconfident.

"Oh, I will study for everything in one day," he boasted, "you just wait and watch."

The night before the test, Hare lay awake all night to study. But he found it difficult to study everything in such a short time. He panicked and got confused, but stayed up, hopping from one lesson to another.

Finally, it was the day of the test. Tortoise, Crocodile and Monkey began writing. They looked very happy because they knew the answers to most of the questions, but Hare hadn't slept a wink the previous night. Alas, five minutes into the test, Hare fell asleep and eventually failed the test.

Don't leave for tomorrow what you can do today.

14 Kenny's Lunchbox

Kenny loved to share his lunchbox with his friends. Every day, his mother would make delicious sandwiches for him. But he never ate them alone. He made it a point to share them with all his friends.

One day, Kenny's mother fell ill. She couldn't make sandwiches for Kenny's lunchbox. That day, everyone shared their lunchbox with Kenny. He didn't go hungry, even though he didn't have a lunchbox.

Sharing is caring.

15 Rob and the Stray Dog

One day, a boy named Rob was returning from school. He saw some children teasing a stray dog. Rob felt sorry for the dog. He went up to them and shooed the naughty children away. The dog then followed Rob home.

Some days later, Rob planted a sapling in a garden nearby. He took care of the plant and watered it every day. One day, when Rob was off to school, another stray dog started uprooting the plant. Rob's dog started barking and shooed the dog away. He saved Rob's precious plant.

One good turn deserves another.

16 Belling the Cat

There once lived three mice – Suzy, Lucy and Tracy, in a king's palace. They lived a very royal life. They would feed on the leftovers from the king's royal kitchen. They were very happy.

One day, the king got a cat named Katie, who loved to chase the three mice. She wouldn't even let them eat the little crumbs that fell off the king's plate. The mice were starving. They met to find a solution to their problem.

"What if we hang a bell around Katie's neck?" Suzy suggested. "She will make a lot of noise when she moves and we'll know where she is. When the bell stops ringing, we'll know she is asleep and we can have a sumptuous feast!"

"Who will do that?" Lucy asked. "Isn't it dangerous?"

"Leave it to me," Tracy declared. She had a brilliant idea.

The next day, Tracy wrapped the bell in a beautiful paper and kept it outside Katie's basket.

"Oh!" Katie squealed. "What a lovely present for me!" Katie wore the bell and the three mice lived happily ever after.

Think of solutions in the face of danger and you will find one always!

17 Nathan's Castle of Playing Cards

One day, Nathan decided to build a castle out of playing cards. He carefully started balancing one card on top of the other. The castle was almost done, when a nasty gust of wind blew the cards down. They fell in a heap.

But Nathan did not give up. He picked them up and started rebuilding the castle. The wind knocked it down again.

This continued till the evening. Eventually, the wind gave up. It stopped blowing and Nathan was able to complete his castle.

Keep trying until you succeed.

18 Judy's Picnic Lunch

One day, Judy and her three friends planned an elaborate picnic lunch for a sunny Sunday afternoon. They spent hours making pies and cookies, and deciding the games they would play. Sadly, on the day of the picnic, it started pouring.

Judy and her friends could have sulked all day about their spoiled plan. But, instead of sulking, they decided to put on their raincoats and sail paper boats in the puddles. The four girls had an amazing rainy day.

Make the best out of a bad situation.

19 The Ant and the Pigeon

One fine, breezy morning, an ant was strolling by the riverside. Suddenly, a strong gust of wind blew the ant into the river. The tiny ant began struggling for her life. Although she swam gallantly, the water current was too strong for her. Tired, the ant started shouting for help.

A kind-hearted pigeon was flying above the river. The pigeon realised that if he didn't help the poor ant, she would drown. He threw a leaf into the water. The ant quickly got onto the leaf and was saved. She waved at the pigeon and thanked him.

A few days later, when the ant was strolling in the forest, she saw a hunter aiming a gun at the pigeon. The ant realised that if she didn't do something quickly, the hunter would shoot. Without wasting a moment, the ant scurried towards the hunter and bit his foot. The hunter lost his balance and missed the aim. The pigeon heard the gunshot and flew away to safety.

Since that day, the ant and the pigeon became best friends.

If you do good to others, others will do good to you.

⑳ Nancy and the Blind Man

One morning, on her way to school, Nancy came across a blind man who was trying to cross the road. Nancy realised that this was a very difficult task for a man who could not see. The blind man was not too sure about crossing the road. He was afraid of getting hit by a car. He kept tapping his stick on the road, but didn't have the courage to walk forward.

Nancy rushed to his side, held his hand and helped him cross the road. The blind man thanked her and she felt very happy to have helped him. Nancy's headmistress was watching this from far away. She was very proud of Nancy. When Nancy reached her class, the headmistress gave her an ice cream as a reward for her good deed. All her teachers and friends also praised her.

It turned out to be the best day of Nancy's life.

An act of kindness never goes unnoticed.

21 Spidey's Web

Spidey the Spider lived in the forest. One winter evening, he decided to spin a web. He got busy with the work. He wanted this web to be big and strong so that many insects would get caught in it through the night. Then he could have them the next day for breakfast. Just when Spidey was halfway through spinning he started feeling tired and lazy. After all, spinning a web is not an easy task.

He was about to sleep in his half-made web when he remembered the story of his grandfather, who had helped King Solomon. King Solomon was inspired when he saw Spidey's grandfather spinning his web and went on to win a war.

Spidey suddenly realised that his task was very simple compared to his grandfather's task.

"I must stop being so lazy and finish my task," he thought to himself. Remembering his hard-working grandfather, Spidey went back to work and spun the stickiest web ever seen.

The web caught many insects overnight and Spidey had a scrumptious breakfast the next day.

Hard work always pays.

22 The Giant and the Baby

A giant once lived on the outskirts of a town. He was almost as tall as a coconut tree. He looked very dangerous with his red eyes and sharp teeth. All the people in the town were afraid of him. No one dared to go near him.

One day, a little baby crawled into the giant's cave. No one thought that they would ever see the baby again. But to everyone's surprise, the giant playfully cuddled the baby and brought him back to his parents.

The people were amazed. They realised that even though the giant looked dangerous, he was actually a very gentle soul.

Looks can be deceptive.

23 Benjamin's Bowl of Milk

Benjamin was a farmer who worked very hard at the farm all day long. One day, impressed with Benjamin's dedication, the owner of a cowshed in the neighbourhood gave him a big bowl of milk. Benjamin was very happy. He was so happy that he started dancing around with the bowl of milk. "Be careful!" cried the milkman. But it was too late. Benjamin, in his excitement, tripped on a pebble and spilled all the milk in the bowl.

Think before you act.

24 The ugly Chick

Once upon a time, there lived a hen in a barn by the countryside. On a Sunday morning, she laid four eggs. Perfectly good-looking chicks came out of three eggs, but the chick that came out of the fourth egg was very ugly.

Everyone in the neighbourhood and at school laughed at the ugly chick, and teased him endlessly. The little chick was very sad.

"I'm so ugly," she thought. "No one likes me. What a waste I am."

One day, the owner of the barn threw a party. Many people were invited. The owner needed three chicks for dinner. He wanted to roast their tender meat and serve it to the guests. He stepped into the barn and chose the three good-looking chicks!

Seeing the fourth chick, he said, "Ugh! If she looks so ugly, how bad is she going to taste?"

And that's how the chick's bad looks saved her from certain death.

Some things are blessings in disguise.

25 The Pixie and the Mosquitoes

Once there lived a very naughty pixie who loved to roam on the streets at night. One night, while roaming, he came across two mosquitoes that were fighting very loudly.

"Everyone knows that my bite is the most painful," said the first mosquito.

"Well, my friend, you are mistaken," the second mosquito yelled. "It's my bite that is the most painful."

On hearing this argument, the naughty pixie decided to intervene and have some fun.

"Hey, you two," the pixie called out. "Why are you fighting over something so silly? Do you see that fat man sleeping under the streetlight? Bite him and we'll know whose bite is the most painful."

The two mosquitoes buzzed off. The first mosquito bit the man on his left hand and the second mosquito bit the man on his right hand. The man woke up startled and slapped his right hand on the left one. The first mosquito died instantly and the second one flew away as fast as it could. The second mosquito realised how stupid they both were to get provoked by the pixie.

Don't act in haste.

26 The Cuckoo Among Cubs

Once there was a tiny error in the admission procedure and a baby cuckoo was admitted to the class of lion cubs.

In the class, the cubs were being taught the art of roaring. But the baby cuckoo could only chirp. The class teacher, a lion, forced the cuckoo to open her mouth and try to roar.

"Roar!" He yelled. "Roar!" The little cuckoo tried really hard till her voice was hoarse. The poor little cuckoo just could not roar, but it couldn't sing melodiously any more either!

Imitating someone without thinking won't get you anywhere.

27 The Crow and the Dove

One day, a crow was flying by a jungle when he came across a beautiful dove. He was so impressed by the dove's white feathers that he also wanted to look like the dove. The crow covered himself with some white paint and started to fly around.

After some time, the white paint wore off. Only uneven patches of the paint remained. The crow was now starting to look funny. Everyone who saw the crow burst out laughing.

The crow had learnt his lesson. He never tried to be anyone else again.

Be happy with who you are.

28 John and the Apple Tree

One day, John was resting under an apple tree. Suddenly, an apple fell on his head. It was a delicious, red apple. After he finished eating it, John saved its seeds.

John took the seeds to his garden and sowed them. He spent hours every day taking care of the seeds. When they sprouted, he watered them, put manure around them and kept all the pests away. His friends made fun of him for spending so much time over it.

He continued to look after the apple plant. After some years, it grew into a tree. John sat under the shade of his apple tree and enjoyed eating the delicious apples that grew on it. He smiled at everyone who had laughed at him.

Prepare today for the wants of tomorrow.

㉙ Jim and the Old Lady

This is the story of Jim, an eleven-year-old poor orphan boy. He earned a living by polishing people's shoes. Jim barely earned enough to buy one square meal a day.

One winter night, when it grew cold outside, an old lady knocked on Jim's door. When Jim opened the door, she requested him to give her some food. She had not eaten for days and looked very weak, too.

Jim had just one loaf of bread that he was about to eat for dinner. He hadn't eaten anything the whole day. Looking at the old lady, he thought that she needed the bread more than he did. He willingly gave her the bread.

As soon as the old lady ate the bread, she transformed into a fairy! She was happy with Jim for being such a good boy. She blessed him with lots of food and riches.

Jim never went hungry after that day.

Good deeds don't go unrewarded.

30 The Sneaky Jackal

A group of lions once caught a very meaty buffalo. They were getting ready for a lavish feast, when a jackal sneaked in. The jackal noticed that the lions were busy getting ready for dinner. He helped himself to a good chunk of the buffalo's leg. One of the lions spotted the sneaky jackal. The jackal was beaten up and thrown out of the den. The injured jackal swore to never sneak into anyone's party again.

Never anger those more powerful than you.

31 Bob's Lies

Bob was a little boy who had a habit of lying. He wouldn't flinch even a little before lying. Whenever he felt too lazy to do his homework, he would lie. He would either say that he was not well, or that his cat was unwell or some other lie. Bob had managed to escape punishment many times by lying. The teacher soon started growing suspicious. How could one person fall ill so often?

One day, Bob couldn't do his homework because he was actually ill. When Bob explained the reason to his teacher, she refused to believe him. She punished him and gave him extra homework.

A liar is not believed even when he speaks the truth.

1 The Thief and Father George

There was a thief who couldn't stop stealing things. He would steal anything that was lying around. He would even pick people's pockets if he saw something he liked. He had stolen little coins from children's piggy banks, dollars from shopkeepers' drawers, wallets from people's pockets and even eggs from a hen's nest.

One day, the thief was travelling by bus. Father George was travelling by the same bus. The thief was standing behind the priest when he noticed a dollar bill sticking out of Father George's pocket. He stealthily pulled it out. Father George was very alert and instantly looked around. He caught the thief red-handed. The thief was very embarrassed and started to look around awkwardly. He thought that Father George would hand him over to the police.

Instead, Father George said, "It's okay, son. Maybe you need it more than I do." Everyone was shocked to hear this. They thought that the Father had let off the thief too easily.

But the thief was very ashamed of his action. He never stole anything from anyone after that incident.

Sometimes, forgiveness is the most effective punishment.

② Dirty Minty in a Fish Tank

There was once a fish named Minty, who was being transferred from the pet shop to a fish tank—her new home. The fish tank was situated in a restaurant and had seven other fish. Minty was very happy to meet her new friends. The seven fish were also delighted to have a new member in the tank.

But Minty had a bad habit. She loved to eat. She ate everything that came her way! She would eat up all the food and the crumbs that children would drop in the tank. She didn't even mind eating tiny insects that drowned in the fish tank at night. She would dirty the tank, too.

The other fish advised Minty to eat less, but she didn't pay attention at all. She continued to dirty the tank. Slowly, she and the other fish started falling ill. When the cleaners came to clean the tank, they found Minty and the other fish ill and very weak.

Your actions affect not only you, but everyone around you, too.

③ The Crane's Breakfast

One morning, a crane was very hungry.
He went down to the river and caught a big fish.
Just then, he saw two small fish playfully swimming
in the river.

The crane decided to balance the big fish in his beak
and hunt the two small fish as well. Carefully holding
the large fish in his beak, he swooped down on the
smaller fish.

Alas, while the crane was doing this, the big fish
slipped from the crane's beak. Hearing the splash,
the two small fish also swam away. The crane had
to stay hungry that morning.

A bird in hand is worth two in the bush.

④ Sally's Dream

Sally was a little girl who was afraid to dream.
She was afraid of being heartbroken if her dream
didn't come true. One day, she saw her friend
describing a beautiful dream. Sally, too, got
tempted to dream that night.

That night, she dreamt of a beautiful blue
blanket. Sally woke up feeling very happy.
To her surprise, her Grandma came to visit
Sally and gifted her the exact same blue
blanket that she had dreamt of!

Sally couldn't stop smiling the
whole day.

Don't be afraid of the unknown.

5 The Hare with One Ear

Once there was a hare named Henry. He got into a fight with an evil jackal and lost an ear. Henry was ashamed to meet his friends with just one ear. He came up with an idea.

He stepped out and said, "Hey friends, did you know that having only one ear is trendy these days?"

All the rabbits believed him and started wishing that they had one ear too. But then, a wise, old hare heard this. He came up to Henry and said, "Would you have said the same thing if both your ears were intact?"

Think before believing tall tales.

6 Rosy the Soap

Once there was a soap called Rosy who was very afraid of being lathered. Rosy was scared that if she got foamy, she would become small in size. Her master was fed up with Rosy because she sat on the shelf like a piece of stone without lathering. Everyone stopped choosing Rosy for a bath. Dust gathered on her.

One day, the shampoo advised Rosy to try getting lathered. The next time, a little girl picked up Rosy. Rosy gave out lots of lather and bubbles. She felt happy and was never afraid of disappearing.

Worrying too much takes the fun out of life.

7 The Monkey and the Sun

One summer afternoon, it was unbearably hot in the jungle. A monkey got very annoyed with the heat. He was continuously sweating. When he couldn't bear it any longer, he jumped off the tree and started yelling at the sun.

"You foolish sun," the monkey said. "Can't you see that you are roasting us alive?"

The sun had never been yelled at, especially by a monkey. He got very offended. After all, he was only doing his job. So he hid behind the rain clouds and began to sulk.

It started raining. The sun continued to sulk and it rained for weeks. Soon the whole jungle became muddy and squishy. There was no sun to dry the water. Slowly, the animals started falling sick. It was then that the monkey realised his foolishness.

"I am sorry, dear sun," the monkey apologised uncomfortably. "Please forgive me." The sun began to shine again. Happy days were back!

Let each one do his job.

27

❽ The Pen and Pencil

One day, a pen and a pencil found themselves sitting next to each other on a desk. It was late afternoon and they didn't have much work to do. They started talking.

The pen asked the pencil, "Don't you feel sad that every time someone uses you, you get shorter?"

The pencil replied, "I felt sad in the beginning. But then, I saw the beautiful drawings that I helped draw and I realised how lucky I am."

Be thankful for what you are.

❾ Phil's Smile

There was a boy named Phil. He loved smiling. He would smile at everyone, even strangers. One Christmas Eve, Santa Claus was getting ready to distribute Christmas presents. Unfortunately, Santa couldn't find his smile. He didn't know where he had kept it.

Suddenly, he thought of Phil. Santa climbed on Rudolf the reindeer and landed at Phil's doorstep. Phil opened the door and gave Santa the largest smile ever. That's how Santa Claus got his smile back!

A smile can go a long way.

10 Smiley the Caterpillar

Once there lived a caterpillar in the forest. His name was Smiley. But Smiley hardly ever smiled. He was sad because he was not as beautiful as the butterflies.

"Why can't I be so beautiful?" He grieved every single day.

One day, he grew tired of looking like a caterpillar and decided to end his life. He climbed on the highest branch of the tallest tree. Smiley looked down from the branch and realised that if he jumped from there, he would definitely die. Just when he was about to jump, a monkey lounging on the branch below called out, "Hey caterpillar, what do you think you are doing?"

"I am ending my life," said Smiley. "I am tired of looking so ugly."

"Maybe, if you waited a little longer, a miracle might take place," the wise monkey said.

"Would a miracle really happen to me?" Smiley asked.

"Oh yes," the monkey said. "Haven't you heard that patience is a virtue?"

Smiley decided to follow the monkey's advice. He decided to wait for a while and to his surprise, he grew into a beautiful butterfly in the next two weeks!

Never give up.

11 The Rabbit's Locked Door

Once a rabbit locked himself out of his house. He was very worried and started struggling with the door. He tried everything, but it was all in vain.

A sparrow came by and asked the rabbit what the problem was. The rabbit explained his problem.

"How will I ever get into the house?" he wailed.

"You see, the window is still open," the sparrow chirped. "You can get into the house and unlock the door from inside."

The rabbit realised how foolish he had been.

Every problem has a solution.

12 The Antelope's Antlers

There was an antelope named Andy. He was rather proud of his antlers. He would stare at their reflection in the pond for hours. "Oh, how intricately are they designed!" he would exclaim.

Then, he would catch the sight of his thin legs and say, "But why are my legs so ugly?"

One day, a lion started chasing Andy. Andy's legs helped him run fast but his antlers got tangled in the low hanging branch of a tree. The lion caught Andy.

What is valuable is often underrated.

13 The Elephant Breaks His Chain

Bingo was a baby elephant when he was brought to the circus. His leg was chained to a strong pole. Bingo tried very hard to break it, but couldn't. He would try to break the chain from dawn to dusk, but would soon get exhausted and go to sleep. The chain just wouldn't break. He soon stopped trying to break free.

Ten years later, Bingo grew up to be a big and strong elephant. He was still in the circus, but was very sad because he was still chained. One day, a sparrow sat on his head and asked him, "Why are you so sad?"

Bingo said, "I wish I could break this chain and be free."

"Oh, but you are so big!" The sparrow looked surprised. "Surely you can break this chain if you want to. Why don't you try?"

Bingo looked at the chain and thought, "That's true. Why don't I?"

Bingo realised that the sparrow was right. He had given up trying to break the chain long ago. He gently tugged it and the chain broke. Bingo was free!

Never give up your independence.

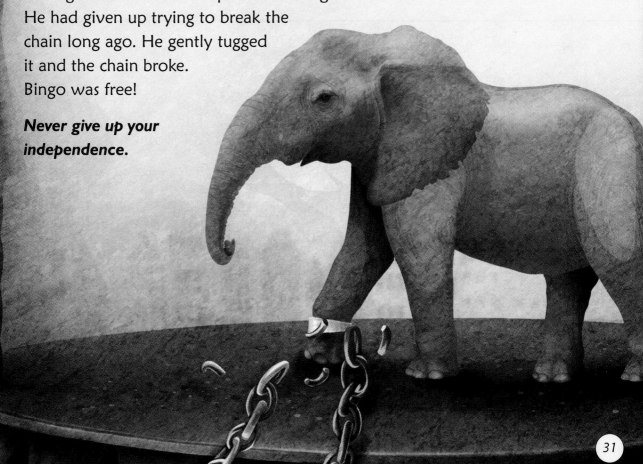

⑭ Wally the Copycat

Once there was a boy named Wally. He was in the bad habit of copying during tests. He would always copy from the person sitting next to him.

One day, the teacher asked everyone to write a formal letter. Wally was so absorbed in copying, he didn't realise that he had copied his neighbour's address on his paper.

When the teacher read Wally's paper, she realised that he had copied the entire letter. He was punished and he failed the test as well. He learnt his lesson the hard way.

Mindless imitation is no good.

⑮ Alana Sprains Her Ankle

Alana was barely eight years old, but she loved to imitate the models who walked down the runway on television. Once, when no one was at home, she got into her mother's high-heeled shoes and started catwalking all around the house!

Since the shoes were too big for Alana, she tripped and sprained her ankle. She had to stay in bed for an entire week and her mother forbade her from catwalking again.

Always act your age.

16 Martin the Engine Goes Off Track

Once there was an engine named Martin. He travelled on the same track every day for years. One day, Martin grew tired of running along the same route. When the engine driver fell asleep, Martin ran off into the field. The ten bogies behind him followed as well. The people in the bogies started screaming.

Martin had a great time running all over the field. On the other hand, the engine driver and the screaming people tried to get him back on track. Finally, Martin was tired. He looked back and was horrified to see the damage he had done! He had destroyed the whole field and many people were very angry with him.

After that day, people refused to sit in the train that had Martin as the engine. They were scared that he would run off into the field again. Martin lost his job. He was then transferred to a train shed, where he sat gathering cobwebs and dust. Martin's good days were over.

Think of the consequences before you act.

17 Alex and His Monkey

A boy named Alex owned a naughty monkey. One day, when Alex was getting ready to go out, the monkey stole Alex's cap and sat on a tree.

Alex tried everything, but the monkey refused to return his cap. Alex came up with an idea.

He put a handkerchief on his head. Like monkeys always do, this monkey copied Alex. It put the cap on its own head. Then, Alex took the handkerchief and threw it on the ground. The monkey did the same with the cap. Alex picked up the cap and walked away.

Quick thinking solves all problems.

18 The Miser and His Bag of Gold

Once upon a time, a miser was travelling by ship. He had a big bag of gold. Suddenly, the ship got caught in a storm. Water started filling into it. In no time, the ship drowned.

The miser was in the ocean with the bag of gold. He didn't want to let go of the bag. After some time, he realised that if he held onto the money any longer, he would drown and lose his life. Reluctantly, he let go of the bag.

Life is more important than money.

⑲ Nancy Reads a Ghost Story

Nancy was an eight-year-old girl who had a habit of reading stories before going to bed. One night, she started reading a story about ghosts. The story was full of evil spirits and demons. Nancy grew very scared after reading the story.

She could barely sleep. She could see a dark shadow moving on the wall all night. The next morning, Nancy had dark circles below her eyes. Her mother asked, "Didn't you sleep well last night, dear?"

"A dark shadow kept moving in my room, Mom," Nancy said.

The next night, her mother decided to find out what the dark shadow was. When they turned off the lights, Nancy and her mother saw that the shadow belonged to nothing but the tree across the street. The shadow moved whenever the tree swayed in the wind.

"Silly girl," Nancy's mother said. "You were afraid for no reason at all. It's just the shadow of the tree!"

Nancy felt foolish that she had imagined so many things just because she had been reading ghost stories at night.

Fear is often just in our head.

20 Four Friends and a Boat

Once, four friends decided to go boating. They went to the riverside and hired a boat. As they were about to get into it, they noticed a sign tacked up. It said that the boat could carry the weight of three people only.

They ignored the instructions and went ahead anyway. With much difficulty, the boat reached the middle of the river. It could no longer bear the weight of an extra person, so it fell apart and sank.

Safety is the first priority.

21 Judy's Dirty Hands

Once there was a girl named Judy. She loved to play in the garden. But she hated washing her hands. Her friends and parents were tired of telling her to wash her hands before eating, but Judy wouldn't listen.

One day, as always, Judy started eating food without washing her hands. This time, some dangerous germs also went into her stomach along with the food and she fell ill.

Judy couldn't attend school or go to play for one whole month. She never forgot to wash her hands after that.

Hygiene should be first priority.

22 The Anthill

Once upon a time, the Queen Ant fell in love with the spot near a pond under a big oak tree. The ants decided to build an anthill on that spot which would be almost hundred times the size of the worker ants.

Each and every worker ant got to work and started planning the construction of this huge and majestic anthill. Just then, a sparrow happened to fly by. The sparrow overheard the plan of building the anthill. He chuckled and said, "You tiny ants are going to build such a great anthill? Is that a joke? You wouldn't be able to complete it in a hundred years!" The worker ants didn't pay attention to the sparrow and continued working. After weeks of hard work, a huge and beautiful anthill was finally ready. The worker ants had succeeded.

The biggest of tasks begin in a small way.

23 The Little Lamb and the Cunning Tiger

One day, a little lamb got lost in the woods. A cunning tiger spotted the lamb. He wasn't in the mood for a chase, so the tiger disguised himself as a sheep and came to the little lamb. "Do you want to play with me? I know of a nice place with a lot of fresh, green grass," he said.

The naïve lamb believed the tiger, who was disguised as a sheep and went along with him. The tiger took the lamb to his den and ate her up. That was the end of the little lamb.

Never trust strangers.

24 The Princess's Necklace

There once lived a very foolish monkey in the jungle. One day, he came across a very beautiful necklace that he had seen around the princess's neck. The monkey was thrilled.

He started showing off the necklace to all the animals in the jungle. When the lion saw it, he got jealous. He decided that since he was the king of the jungle, he should have the necklace. So, he killed the monkey and took the necklace.

Showing off invites trouble.

25 Ginny Learns a Lesson

Ginny was an eight-year-old girl who loved to talk about herself. She would do so for hours, without listening to what her friends had to say.

Slowly, Ginny's friends grew tired of listening to her talk about her dress, shoes, hair, doll and all the other things. They began to avoid her. After a few days, Ginny noticed that no one was willing to talk to her. She realised that maybe she had become too full of herself.

The next day, she sat next to her old friend Rachel and asked, "How are you doing?" Then, Ginny patiently listened to everything that Rachel had to say. Rachel was happy that for once, Ginny didn't interrupt to talk about herself.

Slowly, everyone started noticing the change in Ginny's behaviour and she got her friends back.

A bad listener is a bad friend.

26 Leo Learns to Finish His Food

There was a boy named Leo, who never finished the food on his plate. He would often waste his food and throw it into the dustbin later. His parents were fed up of his bad habit. They put him into a boarding school so that he could be more disciplined.

At the boarding school, whenever Leo sat down to eat, the bullies would snatch his plate. They wouldn't let him eat. Leo went without food for many days. He remembered how he had wasted the food he had at home. He swore never to waste food again.

Value what you have because some day, you may not have it.

27 Baby Bird Learns to Fly

Once upon a time, several little birds were learning how to fly. While all other little birds joyfully jumped off the tree and began flying, one baby bird was afraid of falling down and breaking his neck.

"Well, you won't fall," the teacher bird said. "You know how to fly."

When the baby bird refused to budge, the teacher gave him a gentle push. At first, the baby bird was shocked, but soon, he spread his wings and began to fly.

Don't let fear cloud your instinct.

28 Two Girls and a Bag of Gold Coins

One day, two little girls, Emma and Katherine, were walking down the street. Emma saw a bag full of gold coins. She instantly went towards the bag and picked it up.

"Oh!" Katherine squealed. "We found a bag full of gold coins!"

"We?" Emma questioned. "I was the one who found it. You were looking at the birds. All these gold coins are mine."

Katherine was just beginning to sulk when a genie appeared in front of them. He said, "The person who owns this bag will be cursed!" Emma was taken aback, "Oh, look what we got into!" She whined.

At this, Katherine said, "We? You found the bag and it is yours. So only you are the one in trouble."

Katherine walked away.

As you sow, so shall you reap.

1 The Snail's Journey

A group of snails lived at the foothill of a mountain near a pond. One day, after heavy rain, the water level of the pond started rising. It threatened to flood the area where the snails lived. One snail started climbing the mountain. The other snails laughed. "We are snails," they said. "We are too slow. You will never be able to reach the top. You are wasting your time."

The snail didn't pay any attention to them. He continued to climb. Meanwhile, the level of water in the pond had risen considerably. All the other snails drowned.

The little snail continued to climb slowly. After many weeks, he reached the peak of the mountain. He was safe and sound! The snail was happy and proud of himself. But, when he looked down, he sadly realised that his friends had all drowned.

"If only my friends had believed in themselves," he thought. "They would have been saved, too."

Success comes to those who believe in themselves.

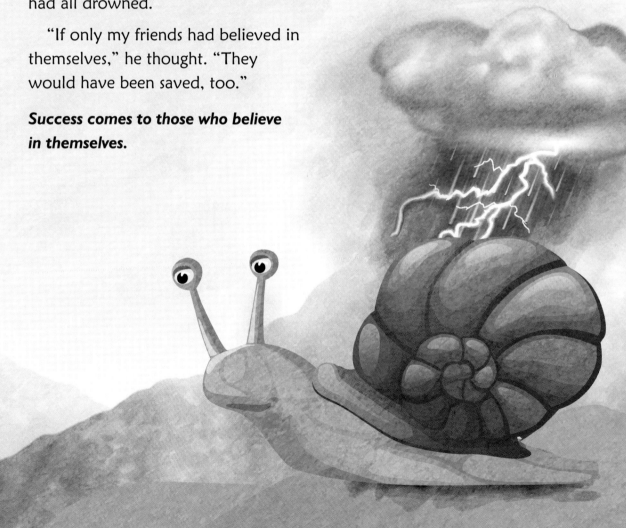

② The Wish Gone Wrong

It was Harry's birthday. He had got many gifts, but he wanted more!

He curled up on the floor and started crying.
A genie passing by felt sorry for him.
He granted him one wish. "I wish for all
the fanciest toys in the world!" Harry said.

Harry showed off his new toys to everyone.
Soon, the whole town knew about his toys.
Thieves got the news and soon began their work.

Every night, some of Harry's things got
stolen. One morning, he woke up to see that
his house was empty! He not only lost his new
toys, but his old ones too.

Be happy with what you have.

③ Julie and the Snake

One evening, Julie was playing in her garden when she saw a snake. She was
about to run away, but she noticed that the snake wasn't moving. At first,
Julie thought it was dead. But then she realised that it was so weak,
it couldn't move.

Julie felt very sorry for the snake. She kept a few eggs near it so that it
could eat. When it had finished eating, the snake slithered
away into the bushes without hurting her.

Julie soon forgot about the incident. But
strangely enough, from that day onwards,
her garden was always free of rats.

Kindness can tame even the fiercest animals.

4 A Fight Between Poe and Joe

One day, two friends, Poe and Joe, got into a fight. They sulked and didn't speak to each other for one whole week.

Finally, Poe went up to Joe and apologised. Joe apologised too. They didn't even remember the reason behind the fight!

Both of them wondered why they didn't apologise earlier. They wasted one whole week sulking when they could have used it to play so many games! They promised each other that they would never sulk for so long in the future.

It's always better to forgive than to hold a grudge.

5 Allan Makes a Sandwich

Allan's mother worked very hard at the office. One evening, Allan decided to make her a sandwich. It was a simple sandwich—just bread toasted with cheese. Allan left it on the table for his mother to eat when she came home.

On seeing her son's beautiful gesture, Allan's mother had tears of delight in her eyes. She was very tired and hungry after a hard day's work at the office. Allan felt happy that he could help his mother in some way.

Good gestures, no matter how small, always count.

6 Emily and the Tooth Fairy

Emily heard that the tooth fairy gave children money for their fallen teeth. When her first tooth fell off, Emily put it under her pillow and waited for the tooth fairy.

That night, the tooth fairy took Emily's tooth and replaced it with a coin. Emily immediately sprang up and looked under her pillow.

"Just one coin?" She said. "You can keep it for yourself!" With those rude words, she flung the coin at the tooth fairy. The tooth fairy was very hurt. She quietly took the coin and went away. She never went back to Emily's house.

Meanwhile, all of Emily's friends kept getting coins from the tooth fairy. Soon, they had collected many coins. They bought lots of things with the money, but Emily had nothing. "serves you right!" said her friends. "You should not have been mean to the poor tooth fairy."

Emily felt bad. She wrote an apology letter and asked her friend to keep it under her pillow with her fallen tooth. The tooth fairy found the letter and forgave Emily. She started going to her house again.

Be thankful when people do you favours.

7 Elsa's Daydream

Elsa was a flower seller. She loved to daydream all the time. One day, she was walking to the market, holding a huge basket of flowers. It was a long walk and she was soon tired. She sat under a tree and rested for a while.

Within no time, Elsa had started daydreaming. She dreamt of how rich she would become if she managed to sell the flowers in her basket. Then, she would buy more flowers, sell them and become very wealthy.

Elsa was lost in her daydream and didn't notice that a group of monkeys had started playing with the flowers in her basket. They threw the flowers and plucked the petals off. One of the monkeys threw a flower at Elsa's face and snapped her out of her daydream.

But it was too late. All the flowers in the basket were destroyed. Now, Elsa's dream wouldn't come true. Elsa realised her folly and decided never to daydream again while at work.

Do not dream when you have work to do.

8 Johnny Spends His Pocket Money

Johnny was excited. He was going to receive his pocket money! He had been saving his pocket money for a month. He was going to buy a toy car with it. He took his money and left for the market.

On his way, he saw an old man selling hats. The old man looked frail and poor, and Johnny felt sorry for him. He decided to spend his pocket money to buy a hat from the old man. He felt sad that he could not buy his toy car. "Oh well," he thought. "There's always next month!"

With that money, the old man had his first meal in days.

Others' needs are more important than your wants.

9 The Lonely Flower and the Bee

There once stood a very lonely flower in the corner of a garden. It had no other flower to talk to.

One day, a bee decided to pay the flower a visit. "Don't worry," said the bee. "You will soon get a friend." The bee said goodbye to the flower and took some of its pollen. It spread the pollen around the flower.

Within weeks, a handful of new flowers sprang up. The flower in the corner of the garden wasn't lonely anymore.

An act of kindness can change someone's life.

⑩ The Penguin and the Orchestra

The jungle animals were starting an orchestra. They were searching for instruments to play. The crab used its claws to pluck at the guitar. The large elephant strummed the big harp with his trunk. Soon, everyone found an instrument to play, except the penguin.

The penguin did not have fingers or claws to play the piano. His body was too slippery to hold the violin. And he could not even fit the flute into his beak! He didn't know what to do.

At last, he went up to the bongo drums and started slapping them with his flippers. What a beautiful sound they made! The penguin finally found a place in the orchestra.

Everyone is special in their own way.

⑪ John and the Little Boy

Every day, while going to school, John would notice a little boy standing outside a sweet shop. He would longingly stare at the sweets displayed at the window. One day, John spoke to the boy. "Why do you stand here every day?" John asked. "I've always wanted to taste some sweets," but I don't have money" said the boy.

John paid for the boy's sweets and fulfilled his wish. The shopkeeper was impressed by John's generosity. He gifted him a bar of chocolate for being so kind.

Kind acts are always rewarding.

12 Tom's Time Changes

Once, here was a naughty child named Tom. He would never respect his elders or listen to them. Instead, he liked to tease the elderly. All the old people in the neighbourhood were very displeased with Tom. But he just didn't care.

One day, Tom saw an old man carrying a very heavy bag of groceries. Instead of helping the old man, he started making fun of his grey hair. Tom stuck his leg out and the poor man tripped. He fell down and his groceries went tumbling everywhere.

Years later, Tom grew old. One day, he was carrying a heavy bag of grocery home when a small boy walked up to him and offered to help him carry the heavy bag.

Tom realised how horrible he had been a long time ago. Instead of teasing the old man, he should have helped him, just like the little boy did.

Tom blessed the little boy and regretted being naughty when he was young.

Treat others like you would want to be treated.

13 John and His Beautiful Egg

There was a boy named John. He found a very beautiful white egg. He was so thrilled to have found it that he kept dancing around and showing it off to everyone. John took good care of the egg and made sure that it didn't crack.

One day, John was so engrossed in telling the story of how he came across the beautiful egg, that he forgot to keep an eye on it. Just then, the egg rolled off the table and broke.

A moment of carelessness can prove costly.

14 The Painting Competition

There was a girl named Tracy. She loved to paint. Everyone appreciated her paintings. But Tracy was very afraid of taking part in painting competitions. She lacked confidence and feared that she could never win.

One day, all her friends got together and made a plan. They sneaked out one of Tracy's paintings and submitted it to a painting competition. The painting won the first prize! It helped Tracy gain her confidence. After that, she always took part in all the competitions she could find.

Confidence and hard work together bear good results.

⑮ The Greedy Mosquito

One evening, a mosquito was feeling very hungry. He started buzzing around a man's ear. After some time, the man got very irritated. "What do you want?" the man asked the mosquito.

"Sir, I am very hungry," replied the mosquito. "I would be really grateful if you let me have some of your blood." The man thought for a moment. "Okay," he finally replied. "But you are allowed to suck blood only from my heel. If I catch you sucking blood from anywhere else, I will kill you."

The mosquito flew to the heel. The skin of the heel was very hard and the mosquito could not get through the skin. Even so, the mosquito didn't complain.

After a while, the mosquito grew tired of trying to suck blood from the tough skin of the heels. He started eyeing the soft skin of the ankle. He just couldn't resist it and stung into the ankle.

The man jumped with surprise when he felt the pain and slapped the mosquito away.

Greed can land you in trouble.

16 The Fairy's Boon

One night, a fairy gathered all the children in a little garden. "Today, I am going to give you all a boon," the fairy announced. "From this day, whatever you think about will come true." With those words, the fairy vanished.

The children were surprised. "Rubbish! Thoughts can't do anything!" One boy remarked and continued thinking nasty thoughts. But the others immediately started thinking of good things. Everyone's thoughts came true, including those of the nasty boy. While his friends got many wonderful things, he got nothing.

Good thoughts bring happy results.

17 The Penguin Who Forgot to Play

There was a penguin named Pablo. He loved to stand first in class and stay spotlessly clean. Pablo spent most of his time studying hard. Slowly, he got so occupied with his studies that he forgot to play. He started losing his friends. They thought that Pablo didn't like them anymore.

One day, an old friend came up to him and nudged him to play a little. Reluctantly, Pablo agreed.

As soon as he slid down the snow, he realised that playing was so much fun! He now understood that playing a little is good for the body and mind.

All work and no play makes you dull.

18 The Lion and the Deer

One day, a lion injured his paw while hunting. He could no longer run fast enough to catch his prey. A couple of days passed and the lion hadn't caught anything except only a few rats.

One day, he saw a deer grazing at a distance. The lion decided to trick the deer so that he could have a decent meal.

The lion started imitating the deer. It looked like the lion was grazing, too! The deer was surprised to see this. After looking at the lion for some time, he could not contain his curiosity anymore. He walked up to the lion and asked, "Why are you eating grass, sir?"

"I think it tastes much better than meat," the lion said. "I know a place with a lot of fresh grass. Would you like to accompany me?"

The deer, thrilled at the prospect of being a friend to the King of the Jungle, happily accompanied the lion. The lion led the deer to his den and trapped him. The deer had to pay for his foolishness with his life.

Trusting your enemies can be dangerous.

⑲ Two Friends and a Sandcastle

Two friends were building a sandcastle on the beach. They could not decide where to put the flag. One friend wanted it on top, but the other wanted it in front. Soon, the argument turned into an angry fight. They were so engrossed in fighting that they didn't notice the waves washing over their sandcastle and destroying it.

When they finally saw the destroyed sandcastle, the friends burst into peals of laughter. The reason behind their fight was now just a large mound of sand in front of them.

Problems come and go,
but friendship is forever.

⑳ Kirk and the Drawing Class

Kirk loved to draw, but he wasn't very good at it. His drawings were so terrible that at times, even the teacher didn't understand what he drew! The other children would laugh at his work.
But he went to the drawing class regularly.

Kirk worked very hard. He practised day and night. He followed the instructions that the teacher gave and saw to it that he didn't let the colour stray outside the borders.

After some months, Kirk took part in a drawing competition. He won the first prize! Kirk's hard work had paid off.

Practice makes perfect.

㉑ No Sleep

Once upon a time, there lived an old moneylender in a small village. He was a big miser. He would lend money to people and constantly worry about whether they would return it! He could barely sleep at night. He spent his whole life worrying about money.

One evening, the moneylender visited an astrologer. He told the moneylender that he would die in a week! The miser was worried. "What about all the money that people have to return to me?" He thought, He did not sleep for the next few nights.

But then, the miser realised that even if people returned his money within the week, he would not be able to spend it! He was going to die anyway. For the first time in his life, the miser stopped worrying. And to his surprise, that week, he slept better than he had ever slept before.

The astrologer's prediction turned out to be false. He didn't die at the end of the week. The miser realised that he would not live forever. He decided to stop worrying about money and started to enjoy his life.

Money is not everything in the larger scheme of things.

22 Suzy Learns to Ride a Bicycle

Suzy always saw her sister riding a bicycle to school. She wanted to be like her. On her seventh birthday, she received a bicycle and decided to try cycling. She was trying to practice riding the bicycle in her lawn, but fell down many times. But Suzy did not give up.

Finally, after practicing from dawn till dusk, Suzy started getting the hang of it. She could finally balance on the bicycle! She loved the feeling of the wind in her hair as she rode down to school the next day.

Keep trying till you succeed.

23 Jake Learns to Swim

One summer, Jake's parents enrolled him for swimming lessons. But Jake was very scared of water. On the day of his first lesson, he was shivering with fear!

Slowly, after days of splashing around, Jake started getting comfortable in the water. He realised that once he stopped struggling in the water, he could float automatically. When he learnt that, Jake learnt to swim within two days.

Success lies in overcoming fear.

24 The Donkey and the Horse

A poor donkey hadn't eaten for days. He was roaming all over the village in search of some grass. He entered a horse's stable. There was lots of hay in the stable. Seeing this, the donkey's mouth began to water.

"Should I eat without the horse's permission?" he wondered, The horse was standing in the corner, munching on his grams. When he saw the donkey, he realised that the donkey was waiting for his permission to eat the hay. The generous horse happily nodded and let the donkey eat as much as he wanted.

A few days later, when the donkey was loitering aimlessly in the pastures, he came across the generous horse again. The horse was carrying some heavy bags of grains. The bags were so heavy that the horse could barely walk. He was huffing, puffing and sweating profusely. The donkey quickly rushed to the horse's side and shared his load. The horse was very thankful to the donkey. After this incident, the horse and the donkey became best friends. They kept helping each other throughout their lives.

Sharing work makes it easier.

25 The School Sweeper

Once upon a time, there was an old sweeper in a school. He did his job very well. The school was always spick and span before the children arrived. Sadly, no one bothered to talk to the sweeper or thank him for his hard work.

One day, the sweeper fell ill and could not clean the school. That day, the school remained dirty all day long. It began stinking. The children then realised the importance of the sweeper's job. When the sweeper arrived the next day, everybody applauded him for his good work.

Always appreciate people's hard work.

26 Mary and the Firefly

Mary was loitering in the jungle when she came across a firefly. She quickly caught it and put it in a glass jar. At first, the firefly struggled to get out of the jar. But it soon gave up and settled down in a corner.

Mary noticed that the light from the firefly was starting to get dim. It was because the firefly was feeling sad and trapped. When Mary realised what was happening, she immediately set the firefly free. The firefly flew away and its light glowed brightly again.

Freedom brings out the best in you.

27 Ann and the Princess Pageant

Ann's school was having a beauty pageant. Ann was poor and didn't have enough money to buy a good dress or a tiara. She went to a seamstress, took all her scrap cloth and made herself a dress. She also crafted a tiara with foil paper and cardboard.

All the judges were impressed with Ann and her clever outfit. Even though the other children had fancier dresses, Ann won the pageant and also won a prize for her creativity.

Creativity solves many problems.

28 Conceited Greg

Greg was a conceited boy who was playing the lead role in his school play. When everyone clapped on the first day, he said, "It's all because of me, I'm the showstopper!" The other members decided to teach him a lesson.

The next day, Greg came to get ready for the play, but no one was there! He was worried. Just before the play, they appeared. They said to him, "What's the matter, Greg? "Aren't you the show-stopper?" Greg was happy to see his friends. He apologised for his pompousness. Once again, they put up a splendid performance. This time, Greg shared the credit with everyone else.

Success never belongs to one person alone.

29 The Talkative Tortoise

The forest was getting flooded and the forest animals had all moved away. But the talkative tortoise stayed where he was.

One day, tired of hearing him complain, two cranes offered to carry him to the mountains. They asked the tortoise to hold a stick in his mouth. Then, each crane held on to one end of the stick and began to fly. As they soared high, the tortoise couldn't hold his excitement. He opened his mouth to speak, but immediately fell down into the water.

Talking too much can land you into trouble.

30 The Fly Goes to a Coffee Shop

One day, a fly entered a coffee shop. He saw many different types of coffees and was tempted to take a sip from them. He started buzzing too close to the cups of coffee. People started getting irritated with the fly and kept shooing him away.

Finally, the fly managed to sit on the rim of a coffee mug, but as he dipped a little to take a sip, his foot got stuck in the sticky coffee. He struggled to escape, but he couldn't. Soon, the fly drowned in the coffee and met his end.

Greed leads to a sorry end.

③1 Molly's Long Hair

Once there was a girl named Molly. She had very long and beautiful hair, and she took great care of it. People would always compliment her hair. All the compliments got to her head. She started teasing people with short hair. She showed off her long hair even more than before.

One day, as she was sitting at a table, a piece of gum got stuck to her hair. Molly tried really hard, but she couldn't get it off. She tried washing her hair and pulling the gum out, but nothing worked.

Finally, she had to go to the hair dresser and get her beautiful, long hair chopped. Her hair that had flowed endlessly now barely reached her shoulders.

Molly realised that all her pride was false. She had hurt many of her good friends because of it. Molly learnt her lesson. She was never proud or haughty again.

Pride keeps us from caring for others.

1 Sally Loses Her Way

Little Sally was on her way to see her darling grandmother. On the way, she had to pass through a big, dark forest. Although Sally's mother had given her clear instructions on how to find the way, Sally got lost. There were so many trees in the forest and they all looked the same! She could not remember her mother's instructions. Poor Sally was quite lost now. With every step, she seemed to be moving further into the dense forest.

Sally didn't lose hope. She knew that her grandmother was loved by all. Even the animals in the forest loved her, because she brought them goodies every weekend. They would definitely know the way to her grandmother's house.

Clever little Sally stopped and asked a few animals for directions. A jumping monkey pointed her to the right path. A chirping bird helped her at a fork in the path. Finally, a hurrying squirrel led her right to her grandmother's doorstep! Sally's grandmother patted her on the back for her clever idea.

Where there's a will, there's a way.

② The Elephant Learns a Lesson

An ant and an elephant went out for a walk. The elephant started boasting of his size. He said to the ant, "If I fell on you, you would die."

The ant just smiled. "Well, I can hurt you too," he said. "You?" The elephant laughed. "How can you harm me?" As soon as he said that, the ant got into the elephant's trunk and bit him. The elephant was in unbearable agony.

One shouldn't underestimate the power of a clever mind.

③ The Race

Two friends, Jack and Jude, were taking part in a race. Jack was very proud that he could run fast. As soon as the gun was fired, he sprinted as fast as he could. But, just a hundred metres into the race, he started to feel tired and slowed down.

On the other hand, Jude steadily built up his speed. He saved his energy for the last part of the race. When the finish line appeared in view, Jude gave it his all and ran very fast.

Jude won the race.

Slow and steady wins the race.

4 Norman's Apology

Norman was a naughty child. One day, while running around in his father's study room, he bumped into an expensive antique vase. When his hand struck the vase, it fell down from the tiny side table and broke. Norman didn't know what to do. He took a broom, swept up all the broken pieces and threw them in the dustbin.

That evening, when his father came home, he didn't notice that the vase was missing. Norman meekly stood in a corner with his head bowed. After a while, his father sensed that Norman wanted to tell him something. He asked Norman, "What happened, son? "Is something worrying you?" "I committed a very big mistake today, father," Norman replied slowly.

"What did you do?" father's tone was stern. "I broke your favourite vase into pieces while playing," Norman said, his voice trembling.

His father looked at Norman quietly for a while. Then he hugged his son and thanked him for owning up to his mistake. Norman was forgiven when he promised never to run around the house carelessly.

Always own up to your mistakes.

⑤ The Parrot's Mimicry

Once there was a parrot who could imitate all the animals and birds of the jungle. Slowly, this parrot became very popular. Birds and animals from all over came to see his mimicry.

The animals liked him so much that they started paying money to see his act. Soon, the parrot began earning lots of money. But gradually, the luxury started making him lazy. He stopped practicing his mimicry and cancelled many shows.

The parrot lost his fame and soon lost his money too.

Pride comes before a fall.

⑥ The Proud Magician

Once upon a time a good old fairy granted a magician a boon. Now he could perform the most complicated magic tricks very easily. He soon became popular. But he started becoming vain too, and began to misuse his magic.

He started turning people into animals and birds. Sometimes he would also make people vanish. One day, he woke up and realised that all his magical powers had vanished! The good old fairy had taken back her boon.

That was the end of the magician's success.

To get carried away by fame is to commit a grave mistake.

7 Richard's Handwriting

There was a boy named Richard. He was a very bright boy who loved reading. At the age of eight, he had read more books than any other child of his age.

He always knew the answer to all the questions during tests. There was just one problem—He had a very bad handwriting. No one could read his handwriting. Even though Richard wrote all the correct answers, his teacher couldn't read them. She would have no choice but to fail him in the test.

Knowledge is incomplete without clear communication.

8 Roger the Thief

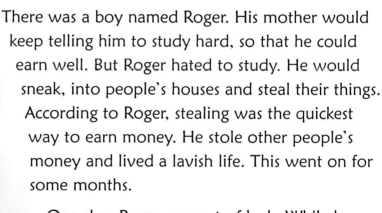

There was a boy named Roger. His mother would keep telling him to study hard, so that he could earn well. But Roger hated to study. He would sneak, into people's houses and steal their things. According to Roger, stealing was the quickest way to earn money. He stole other people's money and lived a lavish life. This went on for some months.

One day, Roger ran out of luck. While he was stealing from an empty house, the neighbours alerted the police and Roger was caught. He spent the rest of his life in jail.

Roger had learnt a lesson the hard way.

Shortcuts aren't always the safest routes.

9 The Bored Rabbit

One day, Bunny the rabbit got bored of the jungle. Ever since he was born, he had lived in the same burrow, played with the same animals and nibbled carrots from the same plant. He was tired of the dullness in his life.

"I want to go to the city now," Bunny said to his friend, Sunny, who also happened to be a rabbit.

"Will you get enough carrots there?" Sunny asked him.

"I will get carrots and many other things, too," Bunny said and set off.

When he reached the city, Bunny was very confused. It only had buildings and roads. He had no place to make a burrow. Just as he was wondering what to do, a group of boys started chasing him. They threw stones and chewing gum at poor Bunny. The gum got stuck in Bunny's bushy tail.

While running from the boys, Bunny fell into an open drain and got covered with filth. He missed his clean and peaceful jungle. He came out of the drain and went back to the jungle. There, he lived happily ever after.

There's no place like home, sweet home.

10 The Frog and the Butterfly

There was a vain butterfly called Flutter. She loved to show off and was very proud of her beauty. One day, she was fluttering over the pond when she met a frog. His name was Croak.

Croak looked at Flutter and his mouth started watering. Suddenly, he had an idea. "Wow, you have such beautiful wings!" Croak said to Flutter. "Will you come closer so that I can look at them?"

"Oh, sure," said Flutter happily. Just as she went near Croak, he caught her with his tongue and ate her up.

Be careful of flattering words.

11 The Cook's Pet Crow

A King's cook had a pet crow. The cook always gave a small portion of the leftovers to his pet crow.

One day, the cook made some delicious fried fish. The crow smelled its aroma and couldn't stop himself from going to the kitchen. When the cook looked away, the crow sneakily took out a piece of the fish. Just as he was about to fly away, the cook caught him. The cook threw him out of the palace and the crow never ate such tasty food again.

Greed always lands you into trouble.

12 Greedy Timsy

Timsy the cat was very hungry. The house was empty because everyone had gone out for a picnic. They would be coming back late at night.

Timsy did not know what to do. Suddenly, she saw some mice playing in the garden. Timsy jumped out of the window and landed in the garden. She saw a little squirrel nibbling at something behind a tree. The mice were playing and running about.

Timsy thought she should leave the squirrel, and attack the mice. This way she would have more to eat. But alas! the moment the mice saw her, they all ran away, squeaking.

The poor cat was left hungry that day. In her greed for more, she did not get any.

Greed does no good.

13 Peter's Rough Day

There was a ten-year-old boy called Peter. He was very upset while walking to school one day. He hadn't completed his homework, he hadn't eaten breakfast and things were not going well for him at school. He had been rude to his friend and now his friend was not talking to him.

While walking past a garden, on his way to school, he saw a little girl sitting on a bench. She was holding crutches and wearing artificial legs. But when she saw Peter, she gave him a bright smile.

The smile changed Peter's day. He decided to smile and apologise to his friend who returned the smile and both became friends again. Peter was no longer sad.

A smile goes a mile.

14 The Curious Monkey

There once lived a monkey who was very curious. Everyone told him to change his ways, but he never listened. One day, he peeked into the kitchen of a house.

Inside the kitchen, he saw a strange object. It was gleaming and had a black handle. The curious monkey jumped into the kitchen and started playing with the gleaming object, not knowing that it was a knife. Suddenly, he cut his thumb on the sharp blade.

The monkey ran away howling in pain. He had learnt his lesson.

Sticking your nose into other people's business is harmful.

15 Grandma's Umbrella

Grandma always carried an umbrella around. She would carry it even when the weather report said that there wouldn't be any rain for weeks. Everyone laughed, but she said, "It's just an umbrella; it doesn't hurt to be prepared."

One day, Grandma was shopping in the market. That day, the weather forecaster had predicted that the sky would be clear. Just when Grandma was about to step out of the market, it started raining. Everyone except Grandma got wet in the rain.

It is wise to be prepared for the unexpected.

16 The Loud Firecracker

Halloween was just round the corner. A group of children wanted to play a prank and have some fun. They came up with an idea for a mean trick. They decided to burst some firecrackers to scare everyone. They bought a large basket of firecrackers and started bursting them in the middle of the night when all was quiet.

One firecracker suddenly burst very loudly and started shooting towards the children! They got the fright of their lives and ran away. Their prank had failed to scare anyone but themselves!

Sometimes, while trying to trick others the joke may turn on you.

17 Two Rams and a Jackal

Two rams who lived in a forest were best friends, though they sometimes argued with each other. One morning, they got into an argument over a petty issue.
A cunning jackal was passing by. When he overheard the rams arguing, he said, "Why don't you two just fight it out? The one who wins the fight will be declared right."

Both the rams agreed. They started hurting each other with their horns. Within no time, they had injured each other badly. But then they realised that they were just acting a stupid and the jackal was making a fool of them. So they both united and charged at the jackal. The jackal ran away as fast as he could, and the rams decided never to fight in front of anyone.

If you fight with your friends, your enemies will take advantage of you.

18 Fairy in the Jungle

A fairy once got lost in a jungle. There she met an evil witch. "You are in my jungle," said the witch. "To get out, you will have to fight me."

"But I don't want to fight," the fairy said. "In that case, you shall remain here," the witch replied. "I was only trying to protect you by not fighting, but if fighting is the only way, then I am ready." They fought and the fairy won effortlessly. Because she was stronger though she did not appear so. The witch disappeared into thin air and was never heard of again.

Looks are deceptive.

19 Ruby Rabbit's Bicycle

Ruby Rabbit's mother bought her a shiny yellow bicycle. Ruby was very proud of her new bicycle. All her friends loved it, too. She allowed them to take turns riding it.

Soon, Ruby noticed that her friends were going out of their way to be nice. Hansel the Hedgehog offered her his chocolate biscuits and Olivia the Otter lent Ruby her pink hairclips. When Hansel and Olivia asked to ride her bicycle, Ruby couldn't refuse. "That's why they were being so nice," Ruby sadly realised.

***Sometimes extra sweet people
have hidden motives.***

20 The Frog in the Well

There once lived a frog named Freddie. He had spent his entire life in a well. For Freddie, the world started and ended in the well. He thought that water existed only within the walls of the well.

One summer, it didn't rain and the well started to dry up. Freddie flew into a panic. He thought that the world was coming to an end.

A wise crow visited the well for a sip of water. "Dear frog," said the crow. "Why are you not shifting to a place with more water?"

Freddie was startled. "What?" he exclaimed. "Isn't this the only place in the world that has water?"

The crow laughed heartily at Freddie's ignorance, but also felt sorry for the poor frog. Had he not come along, Freddie would have died of thirst.

"No, dear frog," the crow explained. "There are many other places that have water and are more beautiful than the one you live in. Pack your bags and get ready to explore the world that lies out of your well."

Ignorance is limiting.

21 The Proud Lion

Once there lived a lion who was a big bully. He bullied all the animals that were smaller than him.

One day, he came across a huge elephant. The lion was unsure about bullying the elephant. But pride blinded his better sense and he started pulling the elephant's tail. The elephant turned and slapped him with his trunk. The lion fell down and realised that even though he was the King of the Jungle, he wasn't invincible.

Pride makes us do foolish things.

22 The Elephant's Dream

Jumbo the Elephant always dreamt about flying. He would see the birds flying high above in the sky. "Oh, how I wish I could fly," he would sigh to himself.

One day, he decided to try flying. He gathered some leaves and made fake wings out of them. He attached those wings to his back and climbed on a rock. He observed a bird taking flight from a nearby branch and tried to copy it. But he fell on his face and hurt himself badly.

Always be yourself.

23 The Herd of Goats

A large herd of goats lost its way in a jungle. A cunning fox saw them. His mouth watered at the sight of such a large herd. He knew he couldn't kill them all, so he came up with an idea.

He went to the goat that was leading the herd and said, "Are you the goats who stay in the village?"

"Oh, yes," the goats said. "Do you know how we could find our way back?"

"Just follow me," said the fox.

The fox took them to the top of a steep rock. "See!" the fox said. "That's your village. If you jump from the rock, you will be able to return to it."

The leader goat could see the village. Without thinking, he jumped down. All the goats blindly followed him without even thinking about it. The fox went to the foot of the rock and enjoyed a hearty meal for many days.

Don't blindly follow the herd.

24 Fish Who Swam into Danger

A big shoal of fish lived in an ocean. The fish didn't even know that man existed. One day, the fish were approached by a turtle who had travelled the whole world.

"Don't go ahead," he warned. "The men have laid a net to catch you all."

"Men?" a fish asked. "There's nothing called men in this world."

While all the fish swam ahead, one little fish stayed back.

As warned by the turtle, the area had been discovered by fishermen, who had spread a strong net. The ignorant fish paid no attention to the turtle's words and swam right into the net. The little fish with the courage to break away from the group was the only fish that stayed alive.

All the other fish were captured and the fishermen enjoyed eating them for dinner.

Always heed the words of those wiser than you.

25 The Boy Who Lied

There was a boy named Danny. He had a nasty habit of lying.

One night, a fairy visited him in his dreams. "You have been lying too much. From tomorrow, whatever you lie, will come true," she said.

When Danny woke up, he decided not to worry about the dream. He didn't want to go to school. "My stomach is aching," he told his mother. "I won't be able to go to school." Sure enough, Danny's stomach actually started aching. He spent the whole day in pain.

Sometimes what you say, actually happens. Be careful with you words.

26 The Rabbit Who Wore Spectacles

A little rabbit loved to play video games. His habit of playing for hours together had strained his eyes. After some days, the rabbit couldn't see clearly. When the rabbit went to the doctor, he was told that his eyesight had become weak. He would have to wear spectacles. Rabbits have very powerful vision and no rabbit had ever needed spectacles before. All his friends laughed at him for wearing spectacles.

The overuse of anything is harmful for health.

27 The Lonely Ghost

There once lived a lonely ghost in an isolated mansion. He was very sad because no one ever played with him. One day, another ghost paid him a visit.

"Why are you so lonely?" the visiting ghost asked.

"I wasn't always lonely," the ghost said. "Once, there lived a lovely family in this mansion to keep me company. They were wonderful people. But I was very naughty and I kept troubling them. So they moved away. I have been lonely since then."

People will move away from you if you trouble them.

28 The Starving Spider

There was once a lazy spider. He was so lazy that he always wove a very tiny web. His webs barely had any place for an insect to get caught.

The spider went hungry for days and started losing weight. One day, an old spider visited the lazy spider and showed concern. "Work harder, son," the old spider said. "And you will be able to lead a good life."

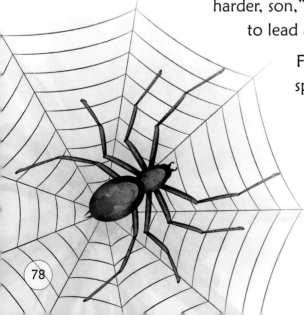

For once, the spider listened to the old spider and spun a bigger web that caught many insects. He promised never to be lazy again.

Hard work reaps rewards.

29 The Nosy Squirrel

There was a squirrel who loved to go sniffing all over the place. Her friends kept warning her that this habit would get her into trouble, but it was all in vain.

Once the squirrel entered a kitchen where the owner had kept some freshly-ground pepper. As was her habit, the squirrel went and sniffed it. All the pepper went into her nose and she sneezed for one whole week. The squirrel learnt her lesson. From that day, she kept her nose out of everyone's way!

Poking your nose into someone else's business is harmful.

30 The Tale of Two Ants

There once lived two ants named Happy and Whiny. Happy went about her day with a smile, but Whiny complained about every single thing.

One day, Whiny asked Happy, "How is it that you find the energy to do so many things without getting tired at the end of the day?"

Happy smiled and replied, "If you conserve the energy that you use in whining and put it to good use, even you won't feel tired."

Whiny followed Happy's advice. She realised that Happy was indeed right!

Don't waste your time whining.

1 Grumbling Uncle Jim

Uncle Jim stayed in a neighbourhood that didn't have many plants. He hated that neighbourhood. Instead of doing something about it, he continued to grumble about the lack of greenery.

One day, two children got fed up of listening to Uncle Jim grumble all the time. They brought a dozen saplings and planted all of them in the neighbourhood. In a month, the saplings grew and the neighbourhood started looking green. Uncle Jim felt bad that he hadn't thought about it first.

Stop whining and start doing.

2 The Man Who Cut a Tree

A man did not like the big banyan tree that grew in his garden. He thought it was very ugly. One day, he took an axe and cut the banyan tree.

But the man didn't realise that the tree wasn't the only one to die. It was home to several birds and insects that helped the flowers in his garden to pollinate. After a while, the whole garden was nothing but a barren land.

The man had learnt a lesson. He vowed never to cut a tree again.

Beauty is not the only measure of value.

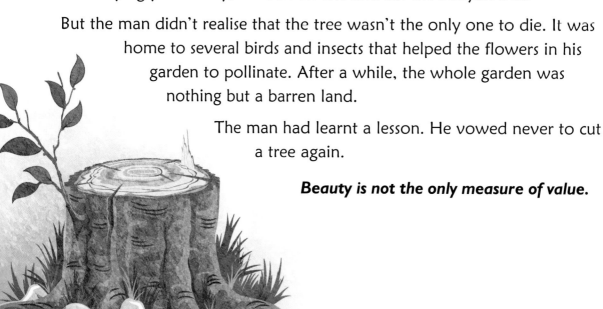

3 The Greedy Mouse

One day, a mouse came across a big block of cheese. The mouse was really greedy and didn't want to leave a single bit of the cheese behind.

With great difficulty, he carried the big block of cheese into his house.

A cat spotted him midway. The cheese was so heavy that the mouse couldn't run fast. The cat caught him easily. If the mouse had not been so greedy, he would have been able to save himself.

Greed can get you into trouble.

4 The Lesson of Cleanliness

There was a group of children who did not keep their neighbourhood clean. They would litter everywhere and never pick up their garbage. Because of this, the locality became a breeding ground for flies and insects. Slowly, all the children started falling ill. When the doctor saw the children, he shook his head. "If you keep your surroundings clean, you won't fall ill like this," he said.

The children started throwing garbage in the dustbins and refrained from dirtying the neighbourhood. Slowly, the mosquitoes and insects disappeared from the neighbourhood and so did all the diseases.

Cleanliness is next to godliness.

⑤ The Painful Picnic

A group of children went for a picnic to a very beautiful garden. After eating and having fun, they left their empty bottles and plastic bags scattered all over the place. Once the children had left, the garden looked dirty and littered.

A dog came by soon after. Unknowingly, he ate a plastic bag. The plastic got stuck in his throat which caused a lot of pain. He had to be rushed to the vet. When the children heard about this, they felt bad. They promised never to litter again.

Be careful of what you do.

⑥ The City with No Flowers

There was a city that was extremely polluted. There were many factories, cars, buses and trucks that released smoke in the air. The people of the city did absolutely nothing about it.

The air above the city was almost black with all the pollution. Slowly, all the birds and butterflies went away. There was no one to pollinate the flowers. The flowers started disappearing. Finally, a day came when not a single flower bloomed in the city. It became the ugliest city in the world. People began to fall sick and started leaving the city to look for a better place to live in. Soon the city was totally deserted and empty.

Correct yourself before it is too late.

7 Duck in the Jungle

A duck lived happily in a lake. She had stayed there all her life. In the same lake lived a crab. He was jealous of the duck's happiness. One day, the crab went up to the duck and said, "Did you know that the forest is a very beautiful place? You must visit it or you will miss out on a lot."

The foolish duck believed the crab's lies and stepped out of the lake. As soon as she stepped into the forest, she got eaten by a lion.

Don't trust people who are jealous of you.

8 Ted's Bicycle

Ted was a very poor boy. He earned money by selling newspapers every morning. One day, Ted thought that if he owned a bicycle, he could go everywhere to sell newspapers. But Ted didn't have the money to buy a bicycle.

Ted didn't lose heart. He started saving a penny every day. Within a year, he had enough money to buy a shiny, new bicycle. With the help of the bicycle, Ted sold many newspapers and became rich.

Saving bit by bit makes you rich.

9 The Foolish Rabbit

One day, Bubba the Rabbit was sleeping under a tree when a pebble fell on his head. He woke up. Bubba thought that a part of the sky was falling. He started running and kept shouting, "The sky is falling! The sky is falling! Run for your lives!"

Many animals and birds believed Bubba and started running with him. The butterfly who was sitting next to Bubba started laughing. "Hold on, friends!" she said. "Don't listen to Bubba. It was just a pebble that fell on his head."

Don't believe everything others say, before first finding out for yourself.

10 Sally's Pink Blanket

Sally loved the blanket her grandma had gifted her. But she didn't take good care of it. She would eat on the blanket and drop breadcrumbs and sauce over it. She didn't wash it for days.

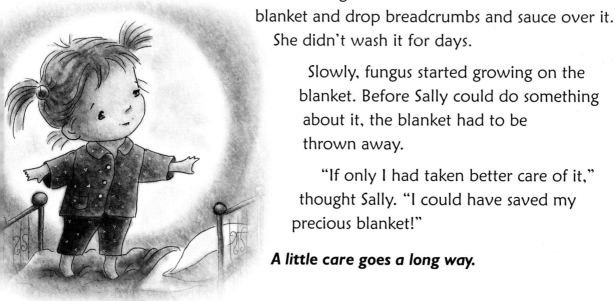

Slowly, fungus started growing on the blanket. Before Sally could do something about it, the blanket had to be thrown away.

"If only I had taken better care of it," thought Sally. "I could have saved my precious blanket!"

A little care goes a long way.

11 The Weak Sapling

There was a weak rose sapling in Henry's garden. He realised that it needed care.

Henry started taking care of the sapling. He looked after it during the day and even at night. He gave it water, manure and lots of love. Within a week, the sapling grew into a strong plant. Henry saved it by taking care of it.

Henry was surprised that he was able to nurse the little sapling back to health with just a little care.

Everyone needs love and care.

12 Grandma Falls Sick

There was once a little boy called Zach, whose grandmother had fallen ill. She was in pain the whole day. Zach started taking care of her. Even though he was little, he made her sandwiches and gave her warm milk.

Zach took care of his grandmother for one whole week. By the end of the week, she started feeling well again. As soon as she could stand up, she went to Zach and gave him a tight hug for taking such good care of her.

You should care for your parents and grandparents, just like they care for you.

13 Weeds in the Garden

Joshua had a very beautiful garden. He played in it every day, but rarely took care of it. Gradually, weeds started growing in a corner of the garden.

The weeds started spreading and took over some of the most beautiful plants in Joshua's garden. That's when Joshua noticed his garden getting destroyed.

He tried cleaning it, but it was too late. All the beautiful flowers had gone. Only the weeds remained.

Laziness is costly.

14 Medicine from Grandpa's Cabinet

One day, Bryan fell ill. He had a headache. He went over to his grandpa's cabinet and took a pill, thinking that it would make him feel better. But the pill that Bryan popped was for a stomachache.

Bryan's headache remained. To add to his woes, he got a stomachache, too! Bryan was miserable and had to be taken to the hospital. After this, he promised never to touch the medicine cabinet again.

Dealing with things you don't know much about could lead to trouble.

15 The Fairy's Magic Potion

Andy wanted to perform well in his exams, but he had a bad memory.

A fairy took pity on Andy and gave him a magic potion. "If you drink this, you will remember every word you read," said the fairy. "But—" Before the fairy could complete her instructions, Andy gulped the potion down.

"But if you drink more than one spoonful, you will not remember anything," the fairy completed her sentence sadly. Alas, it was too late.

Listen carefully before acting.

16 Mike's Late!

There was once a boy named Mike who never arrived on time for anything. He was late for school, late for swimming practice and late to the playground. He was even late for dinner!

One night, an angel visited Mike's dream and said, "Tomorrow morning, at six o'clock, I will distribute intelligence to everyone. Don't be late," she warned. But as usual, Mike was late. Alas, the angel vanished and Mike missed a golden chance.

Punctuality is important or you will end up missing opportunities.

17 The Foolish Woodpecker

A woodpecker was very proud of his strong beak. "My beak can drill a hole into anything," he boasted. An eagle came up to the woodpecker and said, "Will you please come with me? I need a hole drilled into something."

The woodpecker followed the eagle, who took him to an iron pole. The woodpecker didn't know that it was metal. "Drill a hole into this, dear woodpecker," the eagle requested. When the woodpecker pecked on the pole with all its strength, its beak broke.

Pride comes before a fall.

18 Wrong Company

There was a monkey named Juju. He had three other monkey friends. One day, they were sitting under a tree and laughing. "Hey, do you see that big elephant there?" asked one of Juju's friends. "He is a very gentle animal. He won't do anything even if you pulled his tail." Juju decided to try it out.

As soon as he pulled his tail, all his friends vanished. The elephant got angry and gave Juju a good thrashing.

Choose your company wisely.

19 Dogs and Jackals

A dog accidentally got into the territory of jackals. As the jackals moved forward to attack him, the dog's friends joined and protected him. Thus, the dog was saved.

One day, the jackal entered the territory of the dogs. As the dogs began threatening him with growls, the jackal started howling for his friends, but no one came to his rescue. Finally, the jackal had to escape to save his life.

Friends in need are friends indeed.

20 The Hare and the Tortoise

Once upon a time, a tortoise and a hare became friends. One evening, while they were walking in the jungle, they didn't notice that they had come too close to a lion's den. Suddenly, the lion sprung at them. The hare ran away as fast as he could, leaving his friend, the tortoise, behind. The tortoise couldn't run fast. He shrank back into his shell and waited for the lion to go away. When the tortoise escaped, he vowed to be more selective of his friends in the future.

Beware of friends who leave you in times of danger.

21 The Dishonest Milkman

A milkman had to cross a river to deliver milk to the people of the town. Every day, while crossing the river, he added water to the milk. He made a lot of money this way.

One day, the bridge collapsed when he was crossing the river and he lost all his money. As he sat there weeping, a voice from the river said, "Why do you weep over the money that you didn't make? The money was made by selling the water from my river and now the money has come back to me."

Dishonesty always meets a sad end.

22 The Pickpocket's Fate

There was a thief who made money by picking people's pockets on railway stations, bus stops and other public places. One day, he gathered all his money and bought a big diamond with it.

He decided that he would keep it safely in a locker. He put it into his pocket and started walking towards a bank. Just as he was about to reach the bank, someone picked the thief's pocket. Alas, the thief lost all his savings in a moment.

Dishonesty never pays.

23 The Realistic Actor

There was an actor who wanted all his props to be real. If a scene involved swords, the actor wanted real swords. This usually put his manager in a fix!

One day, the actor had to shoot a scene that demanded him to drink poison. "Would you like the poison to be real?" asked the manager mockingly. The actor realised how unreasonable he had been. After that incident, he became much easier to deal with.

Don't make things difficult for everyone by unreasonable demands.

24 The Mighty Lion

One day, a jackal, a wolf and a bear accompanied a lion on a hunt. The lion killed a big buffalo. The jackal came forward and divided the buffalo into four parts.

Before they could start feasting on their shares, the lion cleared his throat. "The first part belongs to me because I led you all," he said. "The second part belongs to me because I killed the buffalo. My cubs need to eat the third part. Now, whoever wants the fourth part can come and fight with me." The bear, jackal and wolf left quietly.

It isn't wise to pick fights with the mighty.

25 The Fox and the Goat

A curious fox was peeping into a deep well. Unluckily, he slipped and fell into it. The fox waited for an animal to come to the well. After a long time, a goat peeked into the well.

"Hey, goat!" the fox called out. "The water in this well is very sweet. Do you want to try some? Come, jump in."

The foolish goat willingly jumped in. The fox climbed over the goat's back and got out of the well, while the goat remained inside.

Think before you trust.

26 The Queen and the Mother Monkey

A queen loved to play with baby animals. One day, she made an announcement in the jungle. "All animals, please get your babies and come to my palace," she said. All the animals left for the palace. Among them was a monkey. On seeing the baby monkey, the queen gasped with disgust. "What an ugly baby this is!" she exclaimed. But the mother just told her baby, "Don't listen to the foolish queen. You are the most beautiful baby."

Every mother thinks her baby is the best.

27 The Hare's Carrot Field

One day, a hare was guarding his carrot field. He didn't let any other hare touch his carrots. He stood there firmly with a stick. Just then, he saw a huge elephant coming towards the field.

The hare looked doubtfully at the elephant and wondered if he should stop the big creature. After a little thought, the hare moved aside and let the elephant eat the carrots. The elephant ate up most of the carrots, but didn't hurt the hare.

If you can't fight, give in.

28 Silly Letty

Letty was a lazy, dim girl who never did anything useful. But she was very vain and proud of her beautiful face. She thought her beauty could make her the queen one day. She would make fun of her friend Rita who would study hard at scool.

It was the day for the school captain to be elected. Letty was confident all girls would vote for her. But she was in for a terrible surprise when the principal announced Rita as the new school captain. No one had voted for Letty.

Letty was horrified. She went home and hid inside a room. She kept crying the, whole day. In the evening she felt lighter and alone. She had realised now that beauty alone does not matter to succeed in life.

Beauty without a good personality is useless.

29 The Foolish Lion

A lion was very proud of his strength. All the animals in the jungle were afraid of him. He ordered that every day, one animal had to come to his den to be eaten. Otherwise, he would kill them all.

The hare didn't want to be eaten. He thought of a plan to stop the lion. On the day of his turn, the hare reached the lion's den very late, looking worried.

"Why are you so late?" the lion roared.

"Your majesty, another lion, who looks just like you, stopped me on the way," the hare said. "I had to save my life and run."

"Is there another lion in the jungle which looks like me?" asked the lion. "Yes sir," the hare said. "He says that he will eat up all the animals."

"Where is that scoundrel?" the lion roared. "Take me to him!"

The hare took the lion to a deep well. The lion peeped in and saw his reflection. He mistook his reflection for another lion and jumped in.

That was the end of the foolish lion. After that, all the jungle animals lived in peace.

There's no use of being strong if you are foolish.

30 The Dog in the Manger

There was once a dog who lived near a manger. Every day, he would see the cows eat hay. One day, he sat right on top of the hay. A cow requested the dog to move so they could eat their hay. But the arrogant dog refused.

The cow complained to the bull who was standing nearby. The bull gave the dog the chase of his life. The dog never dared to enter the manger after that.

Never think the other person is weaker than you.

31 The Arrogant Mouse

One day, two mice were fighting on top of a thatched roof. The strong mouse kicked and pushed the weak mouse. The weaker mouse fell off the roof. The strong mouse was so happy with his victory that he started dancing on the roof.

Far away, a cat spotted the dancing mouse. It pounced on him. And that was the end of the arrogant mouse.

There is always someone who is stronger than you.

1 The King's Nightshirt

There was a very clever thief named Dicey. He never got caught. All the other thieves were jealous of him. They challenged him to steal the king's nightshirt. "He will never be able to do it!" they thought.

To their surprise, Dicey accepted the challenge. He crept into the king's chamber at night, carrying a jar of ants. Dicey opened the jar near the sleeping king's neck so that the ants would get into the king's nightshirt.

On being bitten, the king quickly removed the nightshirt and fled. Dicey won the challenge!

If you're clever, there's always a way.

2 The Crooked Tree

There once stood a very crooked tree in the jungle. It was always sad because it was surrounded by beautiful trees that were very shapely. One day, a woodcutter came to the jungle to examine the trees.

He cut all the trees except the crooked one. "What will I do with this tree?" said the woodcutter, when he looked at the crooked tree.

That's how the crooked tree was saved.

Always be happy with what you are.

3 The Chick That Forgot the Traffic Rules

Once upon a time, a hen was visiting the city with her four chicks. "While crossing the road, look left, right and left. Move ahead only if the road is clear," she explained. All the chicks nodded. It was time to cross the road. Three chicks followed the instructions, but the fourth chick just started walking without looking. She didn't see a truck approaching. The truck screeched and came to a halt. The lucky chick was saved. Then she swore she would always obey her mother.

Listen to your parents.

4 The Jackal and the Foolish Rabbits

A jackal went out to hunt. He came across five rabbits. They had lost their way in the jungle. The rabbits first looked frightfully at the jackal. He pretended to be very innocent and helpful. "I know the way out, dear rabbits," he said. "Follow me."

When the rabbits started following him, he took them into a cave and killed them all.

Trusting strangers without thought could lead to trouble.

⑤ The Camel and the Jackal

One day, a camel and a jackal went into a sugarcane farm. To the camel's surprise, the jackal suddenly started howling. "Shh!" whispered the camel. "The farmer will hear us!" The farmer arrived and started thrashing the camel. The fox ran away and hid.

That evening, the jackal was sitting on the camel's back. When they started crossing a muddy river, the camel bent down and started rolling. The jackal fell into the water and got all muddy.

Do a bad turn and it will return to you.

⑥ The Cat, Dog and the Lion

A dog was boasting about the number of tricks he knew. He asked the cat how many tricks she knew.

"I know just one," said the cat. "Oh! That's it?" the dog said disapprovingly. "Poor you."

Soon, they saw a lion approaching. The cat used her only trick and climbed the tree. She was saved. None of the dog's tricks worked.

It is pointless to be a jack of all trades but a master of none.

7 Bob and the Magical Tree

Bob was wandering in the jungle. He came across
a tree on which a golden fruit was hanging.
He took it home. The next day, Bob found
another golden fruit on the tree.
This happened every day. Soon,
Bob became greedy.

"If the tree gives a golden fruit every
day, there must be a lot of gold in its
trunk," he thought. Bob cut the tree.
He didn't find any gold in the trunk
and he stopped getting his fruits as well.

To be too greedy is to be foolish.

8 The Lion and the Bee

A lion was wandering around the forest. He came across a bee that was
sucking nectar from a very beautiful flower. The lion decided to trouble
the bee. He went near it and roared so loudly that the bee almost fell off the
flower! The lion started laughing loudly.

The bee was so furious, it whistled
and called thousands of its mates.
The lion was stung badly by the
bees. He learnt his lesson.

**Troubling others will only get you
in trouble.**

9 The Boy Who Kept Saying 'No'!

There was a boy who said no to everything. He would always say "no" without listening to anyone.

One day, he went to a friend's birthday party. In the middle of the room, on the table, was the most beautiful birthday cake he had ever seen. It looked very delicious and the boy's mouth started watering. But when the host came and offered a piece of cake to the boy, out of habit, he immediately said, "No." The poor boy went back without eating the cake he so badly wanted because he did not think before speaking.

Think before you speak.

10 The Donkey and the Dog

A donkey and a dog lived in a barn. Every day, when the master arrived, the dog would go to him, wag his tail and lick the master. The master would then play with the dog. The donkey saw this every day.

One day, when the master came home, the donkey went to him, started wagging his tail and even licked the master. The master was furious and hit the donkey with a stick.

Imitating others does you no good.

11 The Shoelaces

Tracy didn't know how to tie her shoelaces. Every day, her mother would tie them for her. Her mother tried teaching her, but Tracy wasn't interested.

One day, Tracy's mother went to the market to buy vegetables and got late. Tracy wanted to go to the playground, but couldn't because her shoelaces weren't tied and she didn't know how to do it.

That day, when her mother came home, Tracy finally learnt how to tie her own shoelaces.

It's always good to be independent.

12 The Year When It Didn't Rain

A forest had a big and beautiful lake. But the animals in the jungle wasted the water. The water in the lake slowly started decreasing.

That year, it didn't rain in the forest. There was hardly any water left in the lake. All the animals realised their foolishness and promised never to waste water again.

But it was too late. By the time the next rains arrived, there was very less water left for the animals. They were thirsty most of the time.

Abusing nature by wasting water could lead to a calamity.

13 The Bully Who Was Afraid of Cats

There was a boy named Tom. He was a big bully. He would always trouble other children and break their toys. One day, the children found out that Tom was very scared of cats. They bought some cats to scare Tom.

The next day, when Tom came to the playground to trouble the children, they set the cats on him. He panicked and ran for his life. He never troubled the children again.

Don't be a bully. It may backfire on you.

14 The Empty Water Tank

There was a girl named Lily. She would never turn off the tap properly. Her mother would always scold her for being so careless, but Lily paid no heed.

One day, like always, Lily left the tap open. That day, her mother forgot to check the taps as well and all the water in the tank was drained out. Lily's family had to face a very tough time without water that day.

After that day, Lily never forgot to turn off the tap properly.

If you keep wasting water, you will not have it when you need it.

15 The Proactive Fairy

God had a lot of fairies to do his work and take care of the world. There was one fairy who did all the work without anyone telling her to do it. She would come up with good ideas to make the world better and was always enthusiastic about all kinds of work. That fairy was God's favourite. When the time came to give away the awards for the year, she got a big prize for being so proactive.

The secret of success is to think of solutions before problems arise.

16 The Overconfident Monkey

There was an overconfident monkey called Coco. He loved to boast about himself. One day, he climbed the tallest tree in the forest and started boasting to his friends that he could jump from the top to the next tree, which was a few metres away.

Coco was too overconfident. He jumped, but he couldn't reach the next tree and fell down on the ground. He broke his hand and refused to climb any tree after that.

Pride comes before a fall.

17 The Grain of Corn

One evening, two hens were strolling in the barn. Suddenly, they came across a grain of corn. They rushed to pick it up. But the corn was too tiny for both of them to pick. They began a fight about whom the grain of corn belonged to.

The fight became too loud and a crow passing by happened to hear it. He noticed that the two hens were too busy fighting to pay attention to the grain of corn lying at a distance. He picked up the grain of corn and flew away.

When two friends fight, a third party benefits.

18 The Tree and the Grass

One day, a huge tree was boasting about its size to the grass. The tree laughed at how small and fragile the grass was. The grass couldn't say anything. The tree made fun of it by saying that everyone walked all over the grass and it couldn't do anything about it.

"Poor you," the tree said. "You are so tiny and helpless."

Suddenly, there was a storm. While the tree got uprooted, the grass remained rooted.

The tree had learnt its lesson.

Strength has nothing to do with size.

19 The Rooster That Partied

One day, a rooster went to a party with an owl. The rooster stayed up till very late and partied into the night. After the party, he went home and slept. The next morning, he failed to wake up on time.

When the rooster didn't crow, the newspaper man, milkman and everyone else continued sleeping. People were late for work.

Everyone was angry at the rooster, who promised never to stay up late again.

Have fun, but don't neglect your duties.

20 The Lazy Sun

One morning, the Sun was too lazy to wake up. When his alarm clock rang, he just turned it off. The Sun turned around and went back to sleep. It remained dark all day!

People were late for work, children refused to wake up for school. Everyone was confused. There was a lot of chaos.

When God came to know about the Sun's folly, he was very angry. He woke the Sun up and shouted at him. The Sun promised never to be lazy again.

It is important to do your work sincerely.

21 The Proud Moon

Thousands of years ago, the Moon became very proud of his beauty and started disregarding the Sun. Even when the Sun rose in the morning, the Moon refused to set.

God decided to teach him a lesson. "The beauty that you are proud of will chip away for fifteen days a month until you disappear. Then, you will reappear," God told the Moon. Since then, for half a month, the Moon gets smaller and smaller every night.

Pride often brings downfall.

22 The Ignorant Rat

A baby rat stepped out of his hole for the first time. He met a rooster with a sharp beak. "*Oh, what a dangerous creature this is!*" he thought and scurried away. He went a little further and met a cat. "*This creature looks so cute with its soft fur,*" he thought. He was about to go ahead and pet the cat when his friend came and dragged him away. "Cats are really dangerous," the friend scolded. "Never go near them."

Looks are often deceptive.

23 The Horse and the Ox

A horse and an ox went to war with their master. During the war, the horse had to carry the master everywhere and had a lot of work. On the other hand, the ox didn't do anything. He just lazed around and teased the horse for working too hard.

When the war got over, the horse relaxed while the ox had to work a lot. Now the horse looked at the ox and smiled.

Bad times befall each of us.

24 The Proud King Cobra

Once upon a time, there was a King Cobra who was very proud of his strength. He slithered all over the forest and scared all the animals.

One evening, while wandering about, he came across an ant hill.

"Why is this hill standing in my way?" King Cobra thought with irritation. With one sweep of his tail, he demolished the hill. Thousands of red ants came out and attacked him. That was the end of the proud King Cobra.

Sometimes the weak can also harm.

25 The Frog and the Lion

Once upon a time, a foolish frog lived inside a well. One morning, he was feeling extremely bored. As he had nothing better to do, he started croaking loudly. He was so loud that he woke a lion sleeping in his den nearby.

The angry lion came to the well. When he saw the frog who had disturbed his sleep, he jumped into the well and scratched the frog with his sharp claws.

Face the music for your actions.

26 The Peacock and the Pigeon

A peacock was very proud of his colourful feathers. He would wander all over the jungle to show off his feathers. One day, the peacock came across a pigeon.

"Oh, you poor pigeon," he said. "Just look at your plain feathers. They look dull and boring. Look at mine, they are so colourful!"

The pigeon replied, "My feathers might look dull and boring, but at least they help me fly. Your feathers are beautiful, but useless."

Useless beauty is nothing to be proud of.

27 The Loyal Mongoose

A family had a pet mongoose. The mongoose loved to play with and listen to the gurgle of the newborn baby, who slept in a cot on the veranda.

One day, the mother realised that there was no bread at home. Her husband was about to come home for lunch. She left the baby in the cot and hurried to the market. As she rushed out of the door, the mother asked the mongoose to take care of her baby.

Just as the lady left, a snake sneaked into the house. The mongoose saw the snake and pounced on it. After a fierce fight, the mongoose killed the snake.

After some time, the lady of the house returned. The mongoose went to the door to greet her. His mouth was smeared with the snake's blood. "Help! The mongoose killed my baby!" she shrieked and started hitting the mongoose with a stick.

Soon, her husband arrived. He rushed in and realised that the baby was still sleeping peacefully. The poor mongoose was hurt for no reason.

Think before you act.

28 The Poor Man Who Was Happy

There was a very poor man who owned nothing. He would eat with whatever alms people gave him and sleep on the pavement under the stars. But he was happy. He had no worries.

One day, a rich man noticed the poor man. The rich man felt bad for him. He gave the poor man a gold biscuit. "Here, you can sell this and earn lots of money," he said.

The poor man had never owned anything so expensive. He went on his rounds and begged, but constantly feared that someone would steal his biscuit. That night, he couldn't sleep at all. He was afraid that if he slept, someone would steal his gold biscuit. All the peace and happiness vanished from the poor man's life.

The next morning, he woke up and went to the rich man. "Please take this gold biscuit back," he said. "I was very happy without it. It has destroyed my peace of mind. I don't want your riches. I am happy the way I am."

Money can't buy everything.

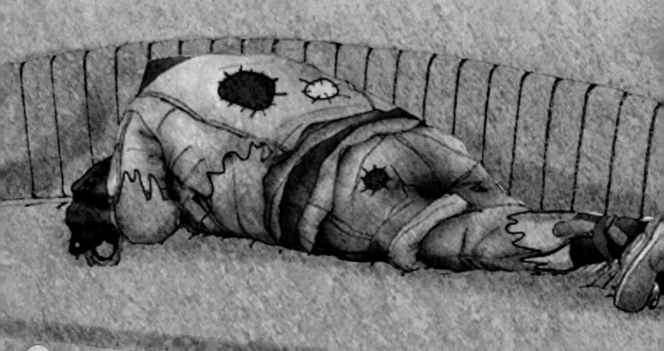

29 The Donkey and the Sculpture

One day, a sculptor hired a donkey to carry the sculpture of a Goddess. As they were walking through the town, many people started bowing and folded their hands in before the sculpture. The silly donkey thought that they were bowing to him! "Let me perform for them," he thought. He started braying and kicking in the middle of the street. The sculptor hit him with a stick. He had made a fool of himself in front of the whole town.

The wise get a nod. The foolish get the rod.

30 The Lazy Donkey

A donkey had to carry salt every day. He carried heavy loads of salt across the river. One day, he lost balance and the bag got wet. Lots of salt was dissolved and the donkey's load lightened.

The donkey was very happy and decided to try this the next day too.

But the next day, the trader loaded him with loads of cotton. When the donkey dipped it into the river, his load became heavier.

Everyone can see through your oversmartness.

① Haughty the Hare

This story is about a hare named Haughty, who was very talented, but afraid of heights. One day, the king organised a big feast for all the hares in his kingdom. Haughty's friends and family were very excited, but Haughty looked worried.

The king's palace was on top of a big hill with very steep sides. Haughty wasn't sure if he would be able to make it to the palace. He tried, but after he went a small distance, his fear got the better of him.

The lights of the palace shimmered at night as Haughty sat at the base of the hill, munching on a carrot.

"I am sure it must be a lousy party. I heard that the food is going to be terrible. Imagine climbing so high only to eat tasteless food. Bah! I am happy here," Haughty said to a mouse sitting beside him.

The mouse looked at Haughty and smiled. "How would you know? You aren't even attending the party and don't have the chance to taste the food. There's nothing wrong with the supper being served at the party, Haughty," said the mouse as he scampered up the hill.

Do not ridicule something just because you cannot have it.

2 The Copper and the Earthen Pots

One day, there was a great flood. Utensils from the house got swept away by the huge waves. An earthen pot and a copper pot were flowing side by side. The copper pot took pity on the earthen pot and asked, "Do you want to hold on to me for safety?"

The earthen pot declined and said, "No, thank you. I am made of clay, whereas you are made of copper. If a wave causes us to crash, I will shatter to pieces and die."

After some time, water filled into the copper pot and it sank, while the earthen pot kept floating.

Strength can be measured in many ways.

3 The Wolf in Sheepskin

A wolf thought that if he disguised himself in sheepskin, he could sneak into a herd of sheep and easily catch a few as prey. He wore the sheepskin and started moving along with the herd. He was just about to attack a sheep when the shepherd called out to his assistant.

"Hey!" he pointed at the wolf dressed as a sheep. "Look how fat that sheep has become! Let's have it for dinner."

The wolf got killed and was eaten by the shepherd for dinner.

Sneaky behaviour always leads to bad endings.

113

4 Two Goats on a Bridge

One day, two goats came face to face on a very narrow and weak bridge built over a river. The two goats could not cross the narrow bridge at the same time. One of them would have to move, but neither was ready to step back.

They started fighting violently and the bridge soon began to shake. Before the goats could realise what was happening, the bridge collapsed and they fell into the river. If they had co-operated with each other instead, they could have crossed the bridge safely.

Fighting is not the solution to all problems.

5 The Cunning Fox

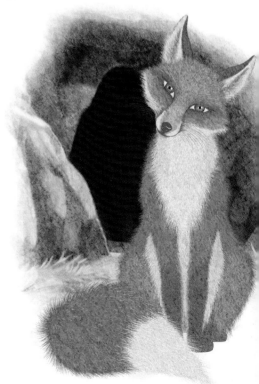

Once a fox had a fish bone stuck in his throat. He went to a crane for help, who readily put his head inside the fox's mouth, down his throat and removed the bone. Now that the fox was all right, the crane said, "Where is my reward for saving your life?"

The fox replied with a smile, "Your reward is that I didn't bite your head off even though it was inside my mouth. Be thankful for that."

Don't expect favours from cunning people.

6 Two Friends and a Bear

Two friends were walking through a jungle when they came across a large bear. One friend quickly climbed up a tree. The other didn't know how to climb a tree, so he used his intelligence and lay down, pretending to be dead. He knew that bears don't attack dead bodies.

The bear came close, sniffed the man on the ground and left. When the coast was clear, the other one climbed down the tree. "What did the bear whisper in your ear?" he asked. "He advised me to stay away from friends like you," replied his friend, who then got up and walked away.

Keep away from friends who will leave you alone in difficult times.

7 The Foolish Astronomer

There was once an astronomer who was very absent-minded. He was always looking at the stars, searching for some sign from the skies. He did not concentrate even while walking! Everyone told him to be more careful, but he hardly cared.

One starry night, as always, he was looking at the stars while walking. Suddenly, he stepped straight into a ditch! He sprained his ankle and had to wait all night for someone to take him out. After this incident, he always paid attention to what was before him.

Reality is more important than dreams and ideas.

8 The Smart Sheep

One day, a wolf caught a sheep. The sheep started shaking with fear, as he did not want to be eaten. Suddenly, he had an idea.

"Dear wolf," the sheep said. "I know you are going to kill me. But will you please honour my last wish?" The wolf considered his request. "Okay," he replied. "What is your last wish?"

The sheep requested the wolf to play him the flute. As soon as the wolf started playing the flute, the sheep dogs traced the noise and saved the sheep.

When you can't fight with your strength, fight with your wit.

9 The Dinner

One evening, a fox invited a stork over for dinner and served him soup in a shallow bowl. Unable to drink from a shallow bowl with its long beak, the stork had to remain hungry that night.

The next night, the stork invited the fox over for dinner and served soup in a pot with a long neck. The fox couldn't drink the soup as its muzzle did not fit down the pot's neck. The fox had to go hungry that day.

Tit for tat.

10 The Naïve Fisherman

A man spent an entire morning fishing, but managed to catch only one tiny fish. Just as the fisherman was about to take the fish home, the fish opened his mouth and began to speak. "You see, I am very small now," he said. "I won't be able to fill your stomach. If you let me live for a few more days, I will grow big and strong. Then you can eat me."

The naïve fisherman set the fish free, but never got it back.

Don't sacrifice what you have for something you may not get.

11 The Cooking Competition

Charlotte and Ben were participating in a cooking competition at their school. Everyone had to make a simple, yet tasty sandwich and salad. Charlotte was busy making her sandwich, when her bottle of sauce fell to the ground and shattered to pieces. She had nothing to put on her sandwich as all her sauce was spilt.

Just then, Ben offered his bottle of sauce to Charlotte. While neither of them won the competition, Ben was applauded for being kind and helpful.

Good deeds never go unnoticed.

12 The Ice cream Seller's Deal

One day, a generous ice cream seller decided to give all the children a treat. "Kids! Come and help yourselves to as many ice creams as you like, all free of charge!"

One greedy boy attempted to carry seven ice-creams in his small, podgy hands. Of course, he couldn't manage this. All the ice creams fell on the ground and were wasted.

The greedy boy didn't get to eat even one ice cream.

Greed will never help you succeed.

13 The Warrior's Sword

There was once a warrior who was too lazy to sharpen his sword. He would keep putting the task off till the next day. But he had delayed it too long. One day, war was suddenly declared.

The warrior tried his best to kill the enemy soldiers, but his sword was too blunt to even cut butter! He couldn't do much to save himself. His laziness eventually caused his defeat.

All the other warriors felt sad for their friend, but also learnt to never be lazy like him.

Laziness is a curse.

14 The Talented Chick

A little chick was good at everything that chicks are able to do. She could sing, dance, act and even balance a book on her head! Her teachers and parents were very happy with her skills and abilities.

However, the chick had a best friend—a squirrel. The squirrel was never happy with the chick because she could not climb trees. The chick wanted to please her best friend. One day, she tried to climb a tree, but fell down and injured her wing.

You can't please everyone.

15 The Boy Who Didn't Pack His School Bag

There was a boy who hated to pack his school bag every night. He would feel too lazy to do it. He decided to go to bed without packing his bag one evening.

The next morning, his alarm failed to ring and he woke up late for school. He rushed through his morning chores and left for school in a hurry.

While packing his bag that morning, he forgot to put his homework in his bag. This caused him to be punished in school.

Procrastination is not a good idea.

16 The Perfect Omelette

Joseph was a little boy who dreamt of making the perfect omelette. When he tried, he realised it was very difficult as the omelette would break every time he tried to flip it.

Finally, after trying hard and practicing for an entire day, Joseph was able to make a perfect omelette. He learnt the right way to flip it. From then on, Joseph's omelettes never broke.

Practice makes you perfect.

17 The Leaking Roof

A lazy man named David lived in a very old house. One day, his wife complained, "There is a hole in the roof, through which the sunlight streams in. Please fix it before the monsoon."

But David paid no heed. Soon, the monsoon arrived and water started leaking from the roof. "Fix the roof or everything in the house will get wet," his wife warned him. Despite the warning, lazy David did not bother.

The hole began to get bigger and finally the roof collapsed. David's laziness had caused the destruction of his house.

Tend to the first sign of damage to prevent a greater loss.

18 The Lazy Cloth Trader

There was a cloth trader who always carried large volumes of fabric in his cloth bag. One day, his bag had a tiny tear, but the trader ignored it and continued with his work. Slowly, the tear began to grow bigger and bigger, till all the fabric he was carrying fell through the hole.

The cloth bag had split open. The trader had to re-stitch the entire bag. He wasted a lot of time and effort.

A stitch in time saves nine.

19 Millie's Laundry

One day, Millie the Mouse decided to dry her laundry out in the open. She began hanging all her clothes neatly on the branch of a tree. Suddenly, Millie saw large, dark clouds looming overhead.

"Oh please, do not let it rain," Millie prayed. "It can rain after my laundry has dried."

After saying this tiny prayer, Millie left her laundry on the branch and went inside the house. Sadly, it rained heavily and all of Millie's laundry was soaking wet instead of dry.

Nature has its rules.

20 The Honest Woodcutter

One day, a woodcutter was cutting wood by a stream. His axe accidentally fell into the water. The woodcutter started crying because he didn't know how to swim so that he could get back his axe out of the water.

Soon, a fairy emerged from the stream carrying three axes – one made of gold, another made of silver and the third made of bronze – and asked the woodcutter, "Which among these is yours, dear man?"

"None," replied the woodcutter honestly. "Mine was an iron axe."

The fairy was so impressed by his truthfulness that she gave him his axe and the other precious ones, too.

Honesty is the best policy.

21 The Story of Two Frogs

One day, two frogs fell into a pot of milk. They both started drowning. They frantically tried to save themselves, but in vain. Finally, one frog just gave up and sank. The other frog went on moving his legs, trying to stay afloat.

After some time, the milk curdled into butter. The frog who did not give up was able to hop out of the pot. His life was saved because he did not give up.

God helps those who help themselves.

22 The Ticket Collector's Loss

A ticket collector liked to watch television until very late at night. One night, he took his addiction too far. He stayed up all night watching television and got no sleep. When he went to work the next morning, the ticket collector felt very sleepy and tired.

As a result, he made many mistakes throughout the day. Because of his poor performance at work that day, he had to pay a heavy fine. He promised never to stay up late at night on a working day.

Early to bed and early to rise makes a man healthy, wealthy and wise.

23 The Mouse Who Knew Karate

A tiny mouse began attending karate classes to learn some moves on self-defence. After just two days of training, the mouse started feeling very capable and confident. He felt like he could fight the mightiest of giants and defeat them.

Filled with much pride, the tiny mouse decided to challenge a lion. The lion had just finished a big meal and didn't wish to eat even a morsel of food. So he spared the mouse's life, but gave him a good thrashing.

The mouse realised how foolish his over-confidence had made him.

Over-confidence could land you in trouble.

24 The Sleepy Fox

There was once a fox who just loved to sleep. If he had the chance to, he would sleep all day long. One morning, however, the fox decided to wake up and get some household work done. He washed all the laundry he had let gather over a week.

He left the wet clothes to dry on the grass and thought, "Let me catch up with some sleep as the laundry dries." And so he went to sleep. After some time, strong gusts of wind blew and one by one, all his clothes flew away.

Carelessness leads to mishaps.

25 The Cow Who Wanted Green Grass

There was a cow who was always in search of greener pastures. If she saw green grass on the other side, she would rush there. Just as she would begin to graze, she would notice the grass a little further looking greener and fresher. The silly cow would move on to that piece of land.

This would go on all day. Finally, the cow would feel too tired to eat anything. This way, the cow went hungry almost every day.

Be content with what you have.

26 The Fat Caterpillar

There was a caterpillar who loved to eat. One day, he kept eating very fast and reached the topmost branch of the tree. As he reached there, he felt very heavy. He could barely move because he had eaten way too much this time.

When he tried to move, he fell through the leaf on which he was sitting, because the leaf couldn't bear his weight anymore. He fell with a thud on the ground and was badly bruised.

He promised never to eat so much and so quickly ever again.

Too much of anything can be bad for you.

27 The Proud Queen

A queen was very proud of her beauty. She placed so much importance on her appearance that she wanted to be surrounded only by beautiful people and things. And so the queen fired all her employees who didn't match her high standards of beauty.

Among those whom she asked to leave was her most trusted advisor. He would advise her on vital matters of governance and administration. Without him, the queen's judgment began to falter and her kingdom was doomed.

Beauty is not the only important quality.

28 The Snail Who Got Left Behind

There was once a snail who ate everything that came his way. His elders and friends would warn him against this habit, but he never really bothered to pay heed.

Once, the entire group of snails went into a field where there was a lot of food. While the other snails ate till their tummies were full, this snail kept on eating and wouldn't stop.

When it was time to move on, the other snails went ahead but this one was left behind and separated from the group.

It is important to exercise moderation in all situations.

29 The Generous Tree

There was a very large and generous banyan tree. It provided shade and shelter to everyone, and swayed gently in the breeze. Several creatures came to rest under its shade and showered it with love.

Many little insects and birds made their homes on and under this tree as they loved its company. The tree now had one big happy family that consisted of so many different species!

The banyan tree was never lonely.

Everyone values generosity and kindness.

30 The Baby Elephant Who Got Muddy

A baby elephant loved to play in the mud. He enjoyed rolling around in it and splashing about all day. One day when the sun set, the baby elephant knew that it was time to go home. But he was so tired that when he reached home, he felt too lazy to wash off the mud from his body. He went to bed just like that.

When he woke up the next morning, his whole body was covered in a horrible rash that stayed for a week! The baby elephant couldn't play in the mud till the rash healed.

Have fun, but be responsible.

31 The Baby Eagle and the Hare

In the forest lived two best friends, a baby eagle and a hare. The baby eagle hadn't learnt to fly yet, so the two strolled on the ground and talked all day long.

Finally, the day arrived when it was time for the baby eagle to fly. "Why don't you also try this with me?" the baby eagle asked the hare.

The two of them climbed the branch of a tree and jumped off. While the baby eagle managed to fly, the little hare fell down and injured himself, as hares can't fly.

It's best to be yourself.

1 The Village Well

There was a village that had not seen good rainfall the whole year. The village well had begun to dry up and its level of water was going down rapidly. All the villagers brought their utensils and containers to store water before it completely evaporated.

There also lived a very lazy man in the village. The villagers knew very well that he would never stand in line to fill a bucket of water for himself. When everyone had finished filling their containers, they left a little water in the well for him.

"Hey!" a villager cried out to the lazy man. "There's still some water left in the well. Fill your bucket before it's too late."

The lazy man thought, "Everyone has already filled their buckets, the water in the well is all mine anyway." And so he didn't bother to collect the water all day.

At night, when he felt thirsty, he fetched his bucket and went to draw water from the well. But of course, there was no water left. The water that the villagers had left for him had evaporated due to the sun's heat. The lazy man was thirsty all night.

It is important to do things in a timely manner.

② The Confused Centipede

There once lived a centipede in the forest who had trouble focusing his attention. Whenever he started walking, his mind would begin to wander. Then he would lose focus and his hundred legs would get entangled. Due to this, the centipede tripped over his legs almost every day.

Fed up of constantly tripping over himself, the centipede decided that he would make more of an effort to concentrate. With each day, he was more successful at walking. Slowly, he mastered the art. The centipede never tripped on his feet again.

You can achieve anything you focus your mind on.

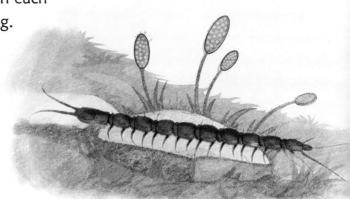

③ The Old Coin

A rich man found an old and worn-out coin in his pocket. He had lots of riches and, therefore, had no need for an old coin, so he left it at the pavement.

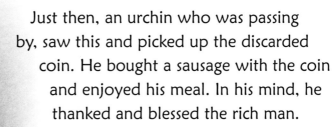

Just then, an urchin who was passing by, saw this and picked up the discarded coin. He bought a sausage with the coin and enjoyed his meal. In his mind, he thanked and blessed the rich man.

Different people value things differently.

4 The Dog's Reflection

A dog was walking by the side of a river with a bone in his mouth. He saw his reflection in the water and thought that it was another dog with a bone in its mouth.

The dog's mouth started watering at the sight of the other bone. He could not control himself. He opened his mouth to snap and bark, hoping to scare the dog in the river. The bone in his mouth fell into the water and flowed away with the river's current. The foolish, greedy dog had lost his bone.

Be content with what you have.

5 The Magic Pen

A lucky man once obtained a magic pen. Whatever he drew with that pen would come to life. The man was very happy. He drew numerous things for his own convenience and luxury. He also drew lots of money so that he could become rich.

One day, he decided to draw a lion for his private gallery. Without thinking about the consequences of his actions, the man drew a lion. The lion suddenly came to life and ate up the man.

Think before you act.

6 The Man Who Won a Lottery

A very lucky man once won a huge sum of money in a lottery. He was very poor and had never seen so much money. When he received the big amount, he didn't know what to do with it.

He splurged most of it on little things that he needed in his home. He still had some money left, so he thought he could try to make more money from the amount he had left.

He went to a casino and played several reckless gambling games. Alas, he lost them all and was left with no money.

Deal with money in a responsible manner.

7 The Mountain in Pain

One morning, the villagers living at the foot of a great mountain woke up in alarm. The mountain was groaning loudly and lots of smoke was coming out of it. The villagers realised that the mountain was in a lot of pain. Not knowing what to do, they started praying fervently.

This ordeal went on for a couple of hours. Finally, the shocked villagers saw a tiny mouse escaping from under the mountain. The reason for all the chaos had been only a little mouse!

Sometimes people make lots of noise over petty things.

8 The Lonely Scarecrow

A scarecrow was feeling lonely. He never had anyone for company. No bird or animal ever visited the field he was in. After months of standing there alone, the scarecrow was fed up of his loneliness.

"Why am I standing here all day when no one needs me?" he thought and left the field.

As soon as the scarecrow was gone, many crows attacked the field and the crops were destroyed. The farmer who had made the scarecrow was heartbroken.

Everything has a specific function or purpose, which cannot be ignored.

9 The Angry Elephant

An ant climbed into an elephant's trunk and bit him several times. Thinking that she had got the better of the elephant, the ant was feeling very proud and pleased. Just then, the elephant threatened to step on her and crush her.

"This big creature has forgotten how much discomfort I can cause him!" thought the ant, as she charged towards the elephant's trunk.

But the elephant had not forgotten. As soon as the ant came close to his trunk, he blew so hard that she flew away and landed at a far distance.

You can't fool the same person twice.

10 The Unsatisfied Butterfly

There was once a butterfly in a garden who loved the nectar of flowers. She couldn't decide the nectar of which flower tasted the best, so she kept hopping from one flower to another and sucked a little nectar from all of them.

However, the flowers got fed up with the restless butterfly and all of them closed their petals to her. The butterfly was forced to leave the garden before she could complete her meal.

Being fussy will get you in trouble.

11 The Careless Boy

There was once a boy who never took care of his skin. He would not apply moisturising lotion when it was winter or sunscreen during the summer. He would also forget to wash his face after getting home.

Slowly, his skin began to crack all over, stinging and hurting him. He had to visit a dermatologist, who prescribed several creams and medicines. The boy later thought that if he had just taken good care of his skin, he wouldn't have had to go through all this.

Prevention is better than cure.

12 The Stray Dog and the Kids

In a friendly neighbourhood lived a stray dog. He would wag his tail and play with the children of the neighbourhood every evening. The children, too, loved to have him as a fun playmate.

On the night of Halloween, some naughty kids decided to play a prank on him. They tricked him by offering him a biscuit, then attached some fire crackers to his tail and ran away. When the crackers started bursting on his tail, the stray dog got really scared and started running. He kept on running till he reached a new neighbourhood.

He felt so sad that he decided never to go back to his old home. The children never saw him again.

Animals too have feelings. Do not be cruel to them.

13 Helpful Larry

Larry was on his way to school early one morning. Suddenly, he heard a cry for help. It was coming from a ditch.

Larry rushed to see who had fallen in the ditch and found that it was Tommy who too was on his way to school. Larry stretched his hand forward and helped Tommy, though he did not like him since he was the school bully.

Not only did Larry's uniform get all muddy, he was also late to reach school. But he had made a new friend in Tommy whom he knew he could always count upon.

Always help others.

14 The Noisy Little Fish

There were two fish in a pond who were creating a lot of ripples in the water for fun. Their families and friends kept warning them to stop being naughty but the two didn't bother to listen to anyone.

Gradually, they drifted towards the shore. The ripples they were creating attracted the attention of a fisherman. Before they knew it, they were caught in his net and fried for his dinner.

Listen to your well wishers.

15 The Wise Boar

There was once a boar who spent all morning sharpening his tusks. Two deer, who were passing by asked, "Why are you wasting your time? There is no one here to fight you right now." The boar said, "Friend, I won't have the time to sharpen my tusks in the very moment that I am attacked. Hence, I am preparing myself now."

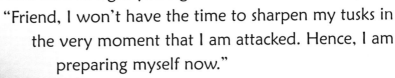

Because of his attitude, even though the wise boar was not the strongest animal in the jungle, he was always well-prepared to defend himself from attacks.

Always be well-prepared.
Do not wait for the last moment.

16 The Thief who turned Over a New Leaf

A thief was caught picking a man's pocket at a bus stop and was sent to jail. There he saw that the inmates were taught to weave so that they could spend their time fruitfully. The thief also started learning how to weave.

Slowly, he became so interested in the process of weaving that he would spend numerous days just weaving yarn. By the time his jail sentence was over, the thief had become a skilled weaver. He turned over a new leaf when he left jail and started his own weaving workshop.

Time is valuable. Utilise it wisely.

17 Long Nails

There was a boy who didn't like cutting his nails. They grew long and when he went out to play in the garden, dirt and mud would get stuck under them.

The lazy boy came home from the park one evening and had dinner without washing his hands. Then he scratched his itchy eyes with his dirty hands. The eyes got infected. Next morning when he awoke, his eyes were red and swollen. He could not attend his friend's birthday party that he was looking forward to. He felt very sad. He promised to keep his nails clean and tidy always.

Cleanliness is next to godliness.

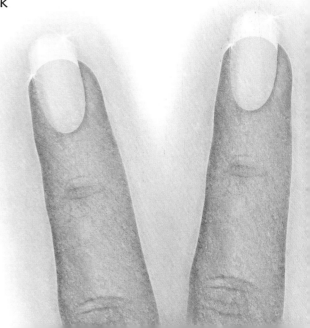

18 Hide and Seek

There was a group of boys playing hide and seek, but they were fighting over who among them would be the seeker. All the boys wanted to hide. They fought, cribbed and yelled throughout the entire evening.

By the end of it, all of them were very tired and sad. They had wasted all their time fighting over a small issue, when they could have spent that time enjoying the game instead. The boys went home with sad faces.

Fighting is just a waste of time.

19 The Football Game

Lucas was playing football with his friends. As he was chasing the ball, James suddenly stuck his foot out in front of Lucas. Before Lucas could react, he had run into James's leg and tripped.

Lucas was angry. He vowed to avenge James's dirty trick. Instead of focusing on the game, Lucas was busy plotting his revenge. He finally managed to trip James, but Lucas had not contributed to the game at all.

Instead of feeling good about his personal victory, Lucas felt that the petty fight with James had not been worth his diminished participation in the game.

Two wrongs do not make a right.

20 The Unjust King

There was once a very powerful king who was also very proud. His arrogance made him punish his subjects severely even for petty crimes. He would spend all his time boasting about his power and might. The people of his kingdom were fed up of this injustice.

They came together to conspire against the king. They united and refused to obey him. The king soon realised that if he wants the people to obey him, he would have to win their love.

Those in power must be gracious.

21 Can a Giant Thread a Needle?

There was a mighty giant who could move mountains with his strength. One day, his frail mother asked him for some help. She needed to thread a needle, but her eyesight was so weak that she could not do it herself.

The giant held the needle tightly in one hand and tried thrusting the thread through its eye. He made innumerable attempts from dawn to dusk, but failed each time. It was then that he realised that not all work can be done with might.

Might is not the only important quality.

22 The Careless Electricity Wire

There was a wire in a town that channelled a great amount of electricity. The lights of the entire town ran on this wire and the wire was very proud of its power. All the great machines in the factories depended on this measly little wire.

One afternoon, the wire was hanging around carelessly, not paying attention to its stray, loose end. Just then, a dog accidentally touched the open end of this powerful electric wire.

The dog was badly hurt. The electric wire was shocked at the pain it had caused and realised its folly.

With great power comes great responsibility.

23 The Rash Driver

This is the story of a man who would not bother about maintaining the car that he drove every day. He was a rash driver and didn't service his car regularly. A mechanic once warned him, "If you don't take care of your car, it will stop working." The careless driver was unfazed. "If and when it stops working, I will repair it," he said. "Why should I bother about it now?"

One day, the car broke down in the middle of the road. The driver took it to the repair shop and the mechanic said, "This car has been so poorly maintained! It is in such a bad condition that it can't be repaired." The driver's carelessness had cost him his car.

A little effort today will go a long way tomorrow.

24 The Bunch of Sticks

A teacher gave each student in class a stick and asked them to snap it into two pieces. All the students easily broke their sticks into two.

"Wasn't that a simple task?" the teacher asked. All the students nodded in agreement.

Now the teacher gave everyone more sticks and asked the students to tie them up in a bundle. "Now can you break them?" he asked.

All the students tried with all their might but no one was able to break the bundle.

There is great strength in unity.

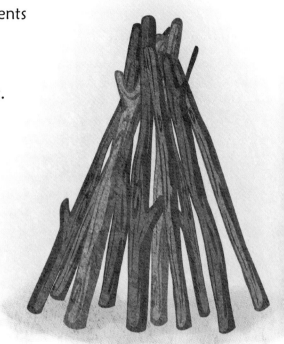

25 A Bell Around the Dog's Neck

There was a man who had a very naughty pet dog. The dog would playfully bite people. The man tied a bell around his neck so that the sound would warn unsuspecting people about the approaching dog.

The dog misunderstood and thought that the bell was a gift from his master. He kept shaking his head so the bell would ring as he ran all over the market. He came across an owl and said to him, "Look! My master is so happy with me that he gave me a bell."

The wise owl replied, "You fool! This bell is an indicator that you are a naughty dog. It is not a gift!"

There is no pride in being known for something bad.

26 The Graceful Crab

Mother Crab was watching her young son learn to walk. He was walking sideways as that is how crabs walk. But Mother Crab was displeased. She caught hold of her son and said, "Walk straight! You must learn to walk gracefully."

Now the son was confused. He had never seen a crab walk straight. So he asked his mother, "Show me how to walk straight. If you walk straight, I will follow."

The mother tried to walk straight, but of course, she couldn't. She had learned her lesson. Never again did she give her son a hard time for not doing something that she could not do herself.

Before berating someone for a task, make sure you have mastered it yourself.

27 The Dog Who Threatened the Ant

A big dog came across a lonely ant walking in the garden. The dog decided to bully the ant, so he went up to her and barked very loudly. This frightened the helpless little ant.

She promptly called out to her friends, who came in the strength of hundreds. They attacked the dog and bit him all over. The dog promised never to trouble any ant ever again.

The ant thanked all her friends for standing by her side in her hour of need.

United we stand, divided we fall.

28 The Snail Who Didn't Do His Homework

There was a classroom full of snails. Amongst them was one snail who hadn't done his homework. When the teacher came to know about it, he took an amusing hat and put it on the snail's head.

"Oh, look!" the snail exclaimed. "This is my reward! I have been so brave by not doing my homework." He proudly showed off his hat to everyone.

All the other snails started laughing at the snail's foolishness.

It is better to be anonymous than to be recognised for something foolish, silly or bad.

29 The Lion and the Boar

A lion and a boar got into a fight. Both were very mighty and strong. They severely injured each other. After hours of fighting, they were tired and sat down to catch their breath.

It was then that they noticed the vultures who were keeping an eye on the two fighting animals. The vultures were waiting for them to kill each other so that they could feed upon their corpses. This realisation brought an end to their fight.

Be wary of sly people who take advantage of others' quarrels.

30 Revenge

A young boy accidentally stepped on a snake's tail. The angry snake bit the boy. The boy's father cut off the snake's tail in anger. The snake killed the father's cattle in revenge.

The father was tired of this vicious cycle, so he said to the snake, "Let's just forgive each other and forget everything that has happened."

The snake replied, "We may forgive, but it's not possible to forget. You will always remember that I bit your son and I will always miss my tail."

Injuries may be forgiven but cannot be forgotten.

31 The Man in the Queue

A man went to the cinema to watch a film. There were several queues outside the ticket office, so he stood in the one that he thought was the shortest. However, after a few minutes, he noticed that his queue was moving at a snail's pace. All other lines seemed to be moving faster.

The impatient man shifted to another queue. But alas! He felt like it too was barely moving. He foolishly spent a long time jumping from one queue to another, instead of patiently waiting to buy a ticket. He missed the movie altogether.

Whatever you don't have always seems more appealing.

1 The Dog Who Wanted to Become Man's Best Friend

Once, a dog came visiting his cousin in the forest. He told his cousin all about Man and how men look after and love their dogs. The cousin decided to leave his home in the forest and move to the city so he too could become man's best friend. When he arrived in the city, he realised that he did not know what man looked like as he had never met one. So he set out to find a man.

During his search, he chanced upon a monkey along the way.

"Is this a man?" the dog thought. He naively asked the monkey, "Are you man?"

"Oh yes!" the monkey replied. "I am man!"

However, the dog wasn't convinced, so he decided to test the monkey. The dog had heard that man worships God. He asked the monkey, "Do you know God?"

Unfortunately for the monkey, he had never heard about God. He assumed it would be a fellow animal and replied, "Oh, yes. I know God very well. He chases the mice every morning!"

The dog had got his answer. He growled at the monkey for trying to take him for a fool!

Lies always get uncovered.

2 The Hare Who Sat Near the Drainage Hole

There was a drainage basin on the banks of a river. All the sewage from the nearby town would collect there before emptying into the river. Because of this, the entire area had a terrible smell.

A hare would come to this spot and spend his entire day just sitting there, in spite of the stench. A mouse once asked him, "Why do you choose to sit in such a smelly place?"

"This is where my home was. I miss this spot as I have a lot of happy memories here." One day the hare fell sick. The doctor told him that cause of his sickness was the polluted air he was breathing. The hare realised his mistake and stopped coming to the drainage hole.

Dwell in the present.

3 The Unfortunate Lion

A mighty lion had been badly injured. He lay helplessly in the forest, slowly dying. All the animals who had always been frightened of him came near him. A monkey came close and cheekily pulled his tail, a donkey kicked his stomach and a mouse nibbled at the skin on his back.

The dying lion could not retaliate because he was weak in his final moments. He lay there thinking, "This is worse than death."

Every dog has his day.

4 The Nurse and the Wolf

A nurse was scolding a boy, "If you don't finish your glass of milk immediately, I will hand you over to the wolf!" It so happened that a wolf from the nearby jungle was passing by the hospital right at that moment. He heard this, so he went and stood outside the window of the boy's room.

This frightened the nurse, who shouted for the guard dogs to chase away the intruding wolf. The little boy laughed at the nurse and the foolish nurse was embarrassed and shamefaced.

Don't make empty promises or threats.

5 The Old Man's Wish

There was a frail old man who worked as a porter. He had to carry heavy loads of luggage every day. One day, he got very tired and said, "I wish I did not have all this work to do!"

His boss happened to be passing by and overheard his employee's lamentation. He promptly dismissed the old man from his job. The poor old man now had no livelihood, all due to a silly remark he had made in a moment of weakness.

Be careful what you wish for.

6 The Man Who Could Read Minds

A man had the power to read others' minds. Initially he used his special power only to help people solve their problems. But soon he became greedy. He began to charge money from people whom he helped. He also cheated them if doing so would bring him more money.

After a few months, he became very rich. However, people soon began to realise that he was unreliable and dishonest. They decided to boycott him and he was no longer respected or popular. Soon, he lost all his money.

The misuse of power leads to downfall.

7 The Weak Baby Stag

There was a rule in the jungle that a baby stag would have to get up on its feet and start running as soon as it was born. If the baby stag didn't run, it would be abandoned by the family.

One day, a baby stag was born in the midst of wild grassland. He stood for a few moments, then collapsed. The other stags moved ahead. The baby stag saw a lion waiting in the grass ready to pounce on him.

The weak baby stag gathered all his strength and ran away.

Survival of the fittest is the law of nature.

8 The Handle of the Axe

A woodcutter needed to make a handle for his axe. He went into the forest and requested the trees to give him some wood. The trees thought, "Oh, what a polite man! Let us help him out." They gave him some wood to complete his task.

Once the handle was made, the woodcutter used the axe to cut down all the trees in the forest. The trees who had given him wood regretted their decision, but it was too late now.

A cunning person will never appreciate your help.

9 The Proud Pen

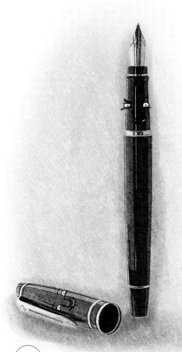

A pen once said to its cap, "You are so worthless! You have no purpose but to sit on my head. I am the one who really has a function to serve." The cap decided to teach the proud and rude pen a lesson, so he hid in a corner. The pen searched for the cap everywhere but to no avail. Slowly, the ink on the pen's nib started drying.

When the nib was so dry that it had become useless, the cap came out of hiding and said, "Now do you realise why I am so important?"

Do not belittle other people, everyone has a purpose.

10 The Thief and the House Dog

A cunning thief decided to break into a house and steal valuable jewels. When he discovered that there was a guard dog in the house, he took some bones to distract him.

When the thief entered the house, the dog charged at him. The thief quickly offered the dog a bone.

"You fool!" the dog barked. "Do you think I don't know your intentions? You have come to harm my master!" The thief was bitten by the dog and handed over to the police.

Do not underestimate your opponents and their intelligence.

11 The Man with Two Wives

In olden times, men were allowed to have more than one wife. There was a man who had two wives – one was young whereas the other was old.

When the man started growing old, the young wife didn't like his grey hair. So she plucked out all the grey hair. The older wife had grey hair herself. She didn't want the man to have only black hair because she thought that she would look like his mother. She plucked out all his black hair.

Soon, the man was bald.

If you try to please everyone, you will end up hurting yourself.

12 Stubborn Sandra

One morning, dark clouds were looming in the sky. Sandra's mother advised her to take an umbrella to school, but she refused.

"If I get wet, I could always dry my uniform. Don't worry, Mummy," she said.

It rained and Sandra's uniform got wet. She stayed in wet clothes all day and caught a bad cold. She had to visit the doctor, who gave her many bitter medicines so she would get well soon.

Sandra regretted not taking an umbrella along.

Prevention is always better than cure.

13 Hardworking Ted

Ted was a young boy who was weak at Math. His friends often teased him for being unable to add and subtract correctly.

Ted started working really hard. He began to focus on the lessons. Slowly, his grasp over Math improved. In the final examinations, Ted scored full marks in Math! His friends never teased him again.

Practice makes you perfect.

14 The Fast Runner

There was a young girl named Darcy who ran very fast. She participated in and won every competition. She once entered a race that was meant for adults, as the running distance was very long. Darcy felt that she would be able to run the great distance and become famous.

Darcy ran but she had pushed herself too hard. She kept running because she was worried that if she stopped, people would call her a failure. Eventually, Darcy fainted and had to be hospitalised for recovery.

Pushing yourself too hard can burn you out.

15 Crocodile Tears

A sly crocodile lived in a river. One day, he saw a monkey strolling by the bank of the river. He crept close to the monkey and started crying loudly. At first, the monkey was alarmed. Sympathetically, he asked the crocodile, "What's wrong?"

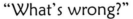

The crocodile cried louder, "I lost my precious stone in the river and can't find it! Will you help me?"

The helpful monkey promptly jumped in to help the crocodile. The crocodile snapped its jaws and the monkey vanished.

Be cautious of people who are not genuine and honest.

16 The Fox in the Storeroom

One day, a fox was wandering through a storeroom. It was very dark in there. The hungry fox started searching for food. Suddenly, he felt as if someone was watching him from the cupboard above.

This frightened the fox. "Could it be a ghost?" He shivered at the thought.

Finally, he mustered the courage to look up. Two eyes were staring at him, but they were attached to a mask. The fox laughed at himself. He had gotten scared of a mask!

Our fears are often unnecessary and trivial.

17 The Lion and the Mouse

A lion was sleeping in the jungle when a mouse ran over his tail and woke him up. The lion caught the mouse in his paw.

"Please let me go, your Majesty," the mouse pleaded. "I promise, I will help you when you need me."

The lion was not hungry and wanted to go back to sleep, so he let the mouse go.

Some days later, the lion was caught in a hunter's trap. Just then, the mouse ran up to the trapped lion. He nibbled on the ropes till they broke away and set the lion free.

Kindness is always repaid.

18 The Rose and the Cactus

There was a garden that was home to a very proud rose. Everyone would admire the rose's beauty, fragrance and softness. Right beside the rose was a cactus, who was not as beautiful as the rose and had many thorns. No one dared to touch the cactus.

The rose started making fun of the cactus. "You are so ugly! Your thorns hurt people. Aren't you ashamed of yourself?"

The sunflower heard this and said, "You should not be so rude, dear rose."

The rose was too proud to care. "Why shouldn't I? After all, this cactus is such a worthless plant!"

Soon, it was summer. It was very hot and the rose started to wilt. It was now too weak to insult the cactus, who was healthy as always.

The rose saw that birds and bees would come to the cactus, suck water out of it and leave. Ashamed, the rose learnt her lesson. Even though the cactus was not beautiful, it served an important function in the plant world.

The rose apologised to the cactus and they soon became friends.

Appearance is not the only important thing.

19 The Greedy Hamster

A hamster was busy storing nuts in his burrow, preparing for the winter. Just then, there was a knock on his door.

"Is anyone home?" a little bird called out.

The hamster was in no mood to entertain guests. Without opening the door, he shouted, "Who is it? What do you want?"

"You see, sir," the bird began. "My wing is fractured, so I couldn't fly south with my family. If I stay outdoors, I will not survive this winter. Could you please give me something to eat and a tiny corner in your home?"

"There's no place in my burrow," the hamster yelled back. "Find yourself something to eat! Don't disturb me."

"Oh, please help me. I'll never forget your kindness," the bird promised.

The hamster finally agreed and let the bird inside. They spent the entire winter together, keeping each other company in the little burrow that they could not leave. To thank the hamster for his kindness, the bird would sing to him every day and even clean the burrow.

People will always be grateful to you if you help them.

20 Rory Rabbit Asks for Help

Rory the Rabbit was being followed by a pack of dogs. He ran for a long distance and tried to dodge the dogs, but was unable to succeed. Finally, he turned to his friends for help.

He first went to his friend Teddy the Bear. "Hey, Teddy! Help me, will you?" Rory asked. "I am being chased by dogs!"

Teddy was sleeping and did not want to be disturbed. He opened an eye and sleepily said, "Go away, Rory, I am too tired to save you."

Rory went to Sam the Sheep's house. "Hey, Sam!" Rory yelled. "Help me please! Dogs are chasing me and I cannot outrun them!"

"I would have, Rory," Sam replied. "But I am busy giving my wool now."

Then, Rory went to Robbie the Robin's nest. "Hey, Robbie! Can you help me?"

"Oh, I'm so sorry, Rory," Robin replied. "But my nest needs some repairing. I must do it right away."

Rory had knocked on the doors of all his friends' houses, but none of them had come forward to help. Finally, Rory hid under the bushes and saved himself from the dogs.

In times of difficulty, you learn who your true friends are.

21 The Greedy Miser

A miser once lost his purse while travelling. He was very upset and distressed, as his purse contained thirty gold coins. He came across a farmer working in a large open field.

"I am finished!" the miser wailed to the farmer. "I have lost thirty gold coins!"

The farmer didn't know how to console the grieving miser. Just then, the farmer's daughter came up to them. She had a purse in her hand.

"Look, father," she said. "This purse has thirty gold coins in it. I found it lying on the road."

The honest farmer immediately returned the bag to the miser, who was greedy and cunning. He said, "Did you say thirty? My purse contained forty gold coins. Where are the remaining ten?"

The miser and the farmer took the matter to court. The judge knew how cunning the miser was, so after hearing both sides, he declared, "Look, you lost a purse with forty gold coins, so this can't be your purse. These thirty coins belong to the farmer's daughter. When someone finds a purse with forty gold coins, it will be returned to you."

Greed will cause your downfall or failure.

22 The Tree That Bore No Fruits

There were two friends who set out to travel on foot and travelled great distances. One afternoon, the sun was bright and hot so they decided to rest under a shady tree.

The two friends lay under the tree's shade. Staring up at the tree's branches, one friend commented, "What a worthless tree this is! It has neither flowers nor fruits."

The tree said, "How ungrateful you are! You are resting under my shade and calling me worthless!" The friends realised their mistake and realised the tree's worth and value.

Be grateful to those who help you.

23 The Man and the Butterfly

A man was strolling in a garden. He noticed that a cocoon was just opening up to release a butterfly. The butterfly was struggling to come out of its tight cocoon.

The man thought that perhaps he should help the butterfly out, so he cut open the butterfly's cocoon. He didn't realise that struggling to emerge from its cocoon was a part of the butterfly's growing process.

Since the man had cut short its opportunity to grow strong through struggle, the butterfly remained weak for its entire life.

A little amount of struggle is necessary for all of us to grow.

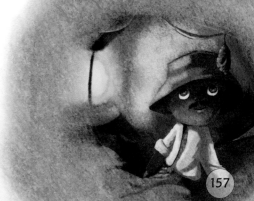

24 The Crystal Ball

There was a village in a mountain valley. All the villagers were poor, but happy. They didn't mind that their houses were made of mud or that they didn't have expensive cars. They were content with whatever they had.

Among them was a boy named John. He had taken his goats to graze one day when he chanced upon a crystal ball with a note that read, *this magic crystal can make wishes come true.*

John wasn't sure what to wish for, so he took the crystal ball to the rest of the villagers, who couldn't contain their excitement. Someone wished for a big house, another for lots of gold and yet another for beautiful clothes.

By the end of the day, the whole village was glittering with riches and luxury. However, the villagers still weren't happy. The one with a big house was dissatisfied as he didn't have gold and the one with gold was upset that he didn't have good clothes.

John observed the unhappy people around him and wished, "Let everything go back to how it was before the crystal ball was found."

All the riches vanished. The villagers were happy again, like they had been before their greed.

Be content with what you have.

25 The Fox In the Tree Trunk

A fox was roaming the forest listlessly. He spotted a village dame from afar. He saw that she was hiding something in a tree. The fox grew curious. He started sniffing the tree once she left.

Lying inside the hollow of the tree trunk was a large, delicious-looking loaf of bread. The fox had never eaten bread, but it looked very tempting. He struggled to go into the tree trunk. He kicked, squeezed and jostled, and even scraped his skin. Finally, he was comfortably nestled in the hollow of the tree.

The fox relished the bread for over an hour. Then he became thirsty. He decided to go to the nearby river to have a sip of cool, refreshing water.

The fox tried to leave the trunk. But now he was stuck. He kicked, squeezed and jostled again, but nothing worked. His short-sighted desire for the bread had landed him in a fix!

Look before you leap.

26 The King Who Started Wearing Shoes

This is the story of a king who had too much money. He also loved to explore new towns and kingdoms. One of his trips involved visiting an extremely beautiful location.

However, this beautiful place was full of pointed stones. The king always walked barefoot. He hurt his feet and they started to bleed. He was furious as he had never endured such pain. He ordered his minister to lay the soft skin of a thousand cattle on the road so that his feet wouldn't hurt.

The minister grew worried. If he were to follow the king's orders, a thousand innocent cattle would have to be killed. He thought hard through the night. He finally came up with a brilliant solution.

He went to the king the next morning. He presented him a pair of shoes made from the hide of a single cow. He minister said to his king, "Dear King, if you wear these, your feet will be spared from all uneven stones."

The king put on his new footwear and walked on the road. He realised that the minister was indeed right. The minister's intelligent and helpful solution had saved not only the king's feet but also a large number of cattle.

Smart thinking is the best option.

27 The Cat Who Didn't Smell the Rose

There was a family who had a pet cat they loved. They gave him fish to eat, milk to drink and a cosy little basket to sleep in. He was a happy cat.

One day, the cat woke up to find that the family had gone off on a picnic. He had nothing to eat or drink. He waited impatiently for the family to return. At the end of the day, tired of waiting, the cat went to sleep in his basket.

The family returned late at night, had their supper and went to sleep in their warm and cosy beds. No one really thought about the hungry, lonely cat.

The next morning, the father woke the cat up to take him for a little walk. While they were in the garden, the father pointed at a rose.

"Oh, what a beautiful flower that is!" he exclaimed. "Kitty, doesn't it smell heavenly?"

However, the cat paid no attention and remained disinterested. He kept sulking until he was served some fish and milk.

One cannot think or act on an empty stomach.

28 The Doll Who Always Smiled

There was a ragged doll that had a smile pasted on its face. A little girl loved the doll very much and would play with it all day long. One day, when the girl was away at school, her mischievous brother got hold of the doll.

"Ew!" he exclaimed. "This is such an ugly doll! I bet it will make a good scarecrow."

He destroyed the doll's neat hair and clothes. Just then, his sister returned from school.

"Hey!" she cried out. "What do you think you are doing?"

"I am using this doll as a scarecrow," the brother said. "Just look how ugly it is!"

The little girl was furious. She snatched the doll back from her brother and said, "So what if it is ugly? It's my favourite doll!"

"But it continued to smile even as I ruined its appearance!" the brother justified.

"Yes," the little girl said. "It is meant to be an example. Learn from the doll how one can smile through life, no matter what one's circumstances may be!"

Always remain cheerful and positive even in difficult times.

29 The Right Time

Ann once put a spoonful of steaming hot porridge in her mouth and burnt her tongue. Her sister Amy said, "Let it cool down for a few minutes. Try eating it then."

Ann replied, "Yes, I will eat the porridge once it's cold." But Amy reminded her that cold porridge tastes terrible.

"If I eat it when it's hot, it burns my tongue and if I eat it when it's cold, it will taste bad!" Ann wailed. "When am I supposed to eat it then?"

"At the perfect time," her elder sister said with a smile.

There's always a right time to do things.

30 Dreams

A grandmother sat by the fireplace telling all her grandchildren bedtime stories. She told them great tales of kings, queens and fairies. The children wanted to enter a dream world as they heard these fantastic stories.

"Granny, we are not able to enter this exciting dream world. Please help us!" the children complained.

"Once you close your eyes, the dream world will come to you. You won't have to go to it. Good night," the grandmother said.

The children closed their eyes and sure enough, found themselves transported to magical lands.

Your imagination can transport you to any place you desire.

1 The Generous Villager

A traveller once lost his way and came upon a village. It was getting dark and he had no place to stay. All the lodges at the village were occupied. The traveller grew worried that he would have to spend the night in an open field. He was afraid that he would be attacked by wild animals.

A villager noticed his concern and said to him, "You are welcome to spend the night in my house." The traveller was instantly relieved. He felt very grateful towards the villager, who had not asked for any money for his kindness.

That night he heard a knock at the door. He heard from behind the curtain a man rudely shouting at the villager. He was asking the poor man to return the money that he had been loaned. The poor villager said he didn't have the money. He stood silently with his head bent low.

The next morning, the traveller gave the villager a large sum of money. "Here, now you can repay your loan. You helped me in my time of need and didn't ask for anything in return. This is my way of thanking you."

Generosity is always returned.

2 When Mother Fell Ill

There was once a boy named Danny who lived with his mother. The mother loved her son very much and worked very hard for him. But one day, she fell ill. She stopped eating and grew weaker by the day.

Danny got very worried and started crying. Just then, a fairy appeared before him and asked, "Why are you crying, dear boy?"

"Oh, my mother is very ill," Danny replied. "She won't eat anything. Please make her healthy again."

The fairy became thoughtful. "That's not in my power. But there is a great mountain nearby. There is a shrub at its peak. If your mother eats the leaves of that shrub, she will be healed."

"Then I will go and get the leaves. Can you look after my mother till I return?" Danny requested the fairy.

"Sure, Danny," the fairy replied. "But the journey to the shrub is very dangerous. Will you be able to go? Won't you be afraid?"

"I will do it," Danny replied confidently. "And I will come back with the leaves."

Danny bravely travelled across the rough, rocky terrain and brought back the magic leaves for his mother. His mother became healthy again.

Success comes to those who are fearless.

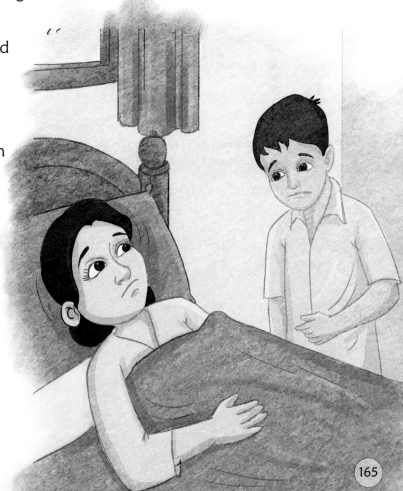

3 The Pig and the Sheep

Some pigs and sheep lived together in a barn. One day, a boy came to take a pig away. The pig started making a lot of noise. The sheep got very irritated with the noise and one of them finally spoke up.

"Hey!" the sheep said. "Why are you creating such a din? The boy takes us, too. Have you ever heard us create such a ruckus?"

The poor pig replied, "The boy fetches you for your wool, but he is taking me for my meat. I am about to get killed."

Be sensitive towards others' circumstances.

4 The Cock and the Jewel

A cock was strolling through a garden in search of a grain of wheat to eat. It combed through the grass and looked carefully under the shrubs, but couldn't find that grain of wheat.

Instead, the cock found a glistening jewel. It was a red shiny stone, which could be worth millions.

"Oh, but what use is it to me?" the cock thought. "It won't satisfy my hunger. It's only the grain of wheat that's precious to me."

Different people value different things.

5 The Fox Who Kicked the Lion

A lion was strolling through the jungle one evening when a nail got stuck in his paw. In great pain, he roared and asked for help. He desperately wanted to have the nail removed, but couldn't do it himself.

He saw a fox nearby. "Hey, fox!" the lion said. "Can you please take this nail out of my paw?"

"Oh, I could," the fox said. "But you will have to let me kick you five times in return."

The lion was furious. He thought that the sly fox was taking advantage of his unfortunate situation. But he was overcome with pain, so he had no option but to agree. "All right," he said. "Kick me if you want."

The fox began to kick the lion, "One, two, three…" he counted. A porcupine was passing by. When he saw the lion's plight, he took out the nail from his paw. The sly fox ran away fearing the lion. The lion thanked the porcupine and both became good friends.

Sly people will take advantage of your unfortunate or troublesome situations.

6 The Pretty Kite

There was a very pretty pink kite. It had a lovely face and a beautiful tail. The children loved it, but they did not know about its shortcoming. The kite didn't know how to fly well. It would bounce from one terrace to another, and was unstable and wobbly in the air.

One day, a child tried to fly the pretty pink kite too high and it got stuck on the roof of a house. The boy pulled and tugged frantically, but in vain. When he managed to loosen the kite from where it had got stuck, the pretty pink kite was destroyed and ripped to shreds.

Looks can be misleading.

7 The Proud Lamp

An old woman would light a lamp in her house every night. The lamp would spread its light in the house and everything would glow. Slowly, the lamp started growing proud. It began to feel like the most important thing in the entire world.

One day, suddenly a strong gust of wind blew and the lamp was extinguished. The old woman managed just fine with another lamp. The proud lamp had learnt its lesson. The next night, when the woman lit it, it stayed humble.

If you are very proud, you will surely be put in your place.

8 The Unreasonable Monkey

There was once a monkey who was making too much noise in the jungle. This was disturbing the birds resting in the trees. For a while they patiently watched the monkey, hoping that he would quiet down shortly. Finally, when he kept making a ruckus, a bird said to him, "Could you please be quiet? We are trying to rest."

The foolish monkey was furious at the bird's gentle and reasonable request. In a fit of anger, he climbed up to the bird's nest and threw it on the ground, so it would smash into pieces.

Unreasonable people do not listen to words of advice.

9 The Spirit of Quarrels

A boy was once roaming the jungle when he came across a bright, shiny ball. When he stomped his feet on the ball in an attempt to squash it, it just grew bigger. He kept stomping his feet on the ball and it kept getting bigger.

A wise old man, who was passing by, said to the boy, "This is the silly spirit of quarrel. If you just let the ball be as it is, it will stay the same size. But if you keep tampering with it, it will keep getting bigger. Don't get involved in quarrels."

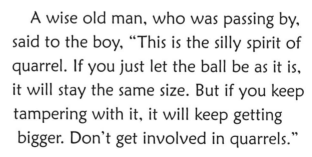

Quarrels can be unending, as they only grow in size.

10 The Pigeons and the Hunter

There once lived two pigeons in the forest. They were husband and wife and loved each other very much. One evening, the wife kept waiting for the husband, but he didn't return. She grew so worried, she went out to search for him.

She found that her husband had been caught by a hunter and was trapped in a cage. The wife went near her husband's cage and started crying. The hunter was about to take her beloved husband away! Just then, it started raining heavily and a cold wind began to blow. The hunter took shelter under a tree.

The wife got an idea. She collected dry twigs from her nest and lit up a fire for the hunter. Then she said to the hunter, "You can roast me on this fire and eat me if you want. But please set my husband free."

The hunter, who was feeling a little warm by now, was moved by the pigeon's love for her husband. He set the husband free and the two pigeons lived happily ever after.

Generosity will always be returned.

11 The Arrogant Swans

There once lived two golden swans in a lake. They were very mean. They wouldn't let anyone else live in that lake.

One day, a duck came to the lake. She liked the surroundings so much that she decided to make the lake her home. Just as the duck was getting her belongings, the golden swans yelled, "Hey! What do you think you are doing?"

"Hi!" the cheerful duck replied, "I am setting up a home here."

"Well, you can't," the arrogant swans said. "This lake is ours."

The duck was surprised. "But this lake belongs to the king. You can't stop me from staying here." The arrogant swans started yelling at the duck. They said, "An ugly bird like you cannot stay with beautiful birds like us."

The duck was furious! He marched off to the king and narrated the entire episode. The king got angry and called for the swans. When the swans arrived, he told them, "How dare you stop anyone from staying on my property? I don't want you to stay there anymore. Leave now or I will get you killed."

That was the last time the golden swans were seen in the beautiful lake.

Arrogance is harmful.

12 Hammering Nails in the Fence

There was once a boy who lost his temper very often. One day, his father told him, "Hammer a nail into the fence every time you lose your temper."

Initially there were twenty nails on the fence per day. Slowly, the number started decreasing. Finally, a day came when the boy didn't lose his temper even once.

But when the father and son removed the nails hammered in the fence, they saw that it had left behind many holes. The son felt bad and promised to control his temper in future.

Anger leaves permanent scars.

13 The Curse of the Bullocks

A farmer once owned a pair of bullocks. He had a very lazy daughter. Once, during summer, when the heat was at its peak, the farmer asked his daughter to take the bullocks to the river.

The lazy girl took the bullocks. But on the way, she saw a tree. She tied the bullocks to the tree and fell asleep under its shade. The bullocks were furious and they cursed the girl. "In your next birth, you will become a bird that drinks only during the monsoon."

And the curse came true!

Laziness can be harmful.

14 The Cunning Bats

There was an election in the forest. The lion and the eagle were competing for the title of the king. The cunning bats wanted to win the trust of both sides. They first went to the lion saying, "We think you are best suited to be the king."

Then they went to the eagle and said, "You are very admirable. Even though the lion appears to be strong, you have the wisdom and grace to be the king of the jungle."

But soon, both the lion and the eagle realised that the bats were cunning. They called all the animals and birds in the jungle and also the bats.

The lion roared and said, "You do not lay eggs and are not like the birds. You are like the animals, so come to our side."

The eagle on the other side screeched, "You fly like the birds, so tell us, dear bats, isn't your place in my kingdom?"

The sheepish bats were embarrassed. Their deceit was exposed. They flew away and hid inside the caves. They were so embarrassed that they never came out in broad daylight after that.

Lies and deceit only brings trouble.

15 The Solution that went wrong

A crane was very upset. A snake kept eating her eggs. She went to her friend, the crab, to find a solution. He had an idea.

The crane and the crab lay a trail of fish from the snake's hole to the mongoose's hole. When the mongoose woke up in the morning, he started eating the fish and reached the snake's house. When the snake saw the mongoose, he thought that the mongoose had come to fight.

The snake and the mongoose fought bitterly and the snake was killed. The crane and the crab thought that their problem was solved.

But the next day, the mongoose again set out to search for fish and reached the crane's nest. There he saw the eggs and ate them up.

The crane and the crab regretted their decision.

Consider the consequences before deciding a solution.

16 The Greedy Farmer

A very greedy farmer had a rich businessman as his friend. One day, the businessman had to leave town for a meeting. He handed his iron box full of valuables to the farmer and said, "Take care of this box, my friend."

The farmer promised to do so. But when the businessman returned and asked the farmer for his iron box, the farmer said, "I am sorry, my friend. A mouse came in and ate it all up!"

The businessman didn't believe a word. He could see that his friend had cheated on him. But he remained silent.

One day, the farmer left his son at the businessman's house. When he returned, the businessman said, "I'm sorry, a hawk carried your son away."

The farmer was furious. "Have you lost your mind?" he cried. "How can a hawk carry off a grown up boy?"

"The same way as a mouse can eat an iron box," the businessman replied with a smile.

The farmer apologised to the businessman and returned his iron box. The businessman then set the farmer's son free.

Do not lie or cheat.

17 The dissatisfied Stone Cutter

There was once a very unhappy stonecutter. Once he looked at the king and wished, "It would be so nice if I could be the king." The next morning, he woke up and saw that he had turned into a king. He wore fine clothes and had a hundred servants at his beck and call. He immediately set off on a journey to a faraway land.

While travelling, he started feeling very hot in all the finery. The sun was too bright. "I wish I were the sun," he thought.

The next morning, he was the sun. He shone as brightly as he could, but he couldn't see past the clouds. "I wish I were a cloud," he thought.

The next day, he found he had become a cloud. But he saw that the clouds soon turned into water and fell on hard rocks on the earth. "I wish I were a hard rock."

The next day, he turned into a rock. When he saw a stonecutter cutting a rock, he thought, "I wish I were a stonecutter."

And the stonecutter returned to his original self. He never complained after that.

Be satisfied with what you are.

18 The Mouse Who Grew Fat

A mouse found a jar filled with cheese. He hadn't eaten much for four days and had grown frail and weak. When he opened the lid of the jar, he easily got in because of his size.

He ate the cheese for a whole week and finished everything in the jar. Now, he felt full and satisfied. When he tried to move out of the jar, he realised that he had grown fat. He was too fat to get out of the jar! The mouse was stuck in there for days.

Think before you act.

19 The Donkey's Shadow

John once hired a donkey from Tom. John, Tom and the donkey were walking in the afternoon when the sun started shining very brightly. John and Tom stood under the donkey's shadow. But the shadow grew shorter and John started pushing Tom out.

"I have paid the rent for the donkey, so I will stand in its shadow," John reasoned.

"You paid for the donkey, not for its shadow," Tom retorted.

While the two were fighting, Tom's elbow jabbed into the donkey and it ran away, leaving the two men behind.

Keep the consequences of your actions in mind.

20 The Man Who Helped the Eagle

A man found an eagle with a broken wing. He nursed her until she was healthy enough to fly away.

After a few months, the man was walking alongside a great stone wall. The same eagle saw the man from far. She swooped down, caught the man's hat in her claws and threw it far away. The man ran after his hat. Just as he was about to pick it up, the stone wall collapsed. The man thanked the eagle.

If you help others, others will help you.

21 Monkey in the Net

A monkey was sitting by the river bank when he saw a fisherman spreading the net to catch some fish. The fisherman spread the net wide. When he removed the net, there were many fish in it.

The monkey was impressed. When the fisherman went for lunch, leaving the net behind, the monkey tried to imitate his actions. But he got tangled in the net and fell in the river. The foolish monkey was rescued when the fisherman returned after lunch.

Foolish imitations can be dangerous.

22 The Monkey and the Crocodile

There once lived a crocodile in a river. On one bank of the river was an apple tree. One morning, the crocodile was longingly looking at a juicy apple. "I wish I could eat that," he thought aloud. Just then, a monkey appeared, plucked the apple and threw it at the crocodile.

They soon became good friends. Seeing their friendship, the crocodile's wife got jealous. She told him, "The heart of a monkey who eats such sweet and juicy apples would be so sweet! I want to eat his heart!"

The crocodile tried to convince his wife, but in vain. Finally, he went to the monkey and said, "Come friend, let me take you for a ride." The monkey happily hopped on. In the middle of the river, the crocodile told him the entire story.

"Oh!" the monkey exclaimed, "you should have told me earlier. I left my heart on the tree."

The foolish crocodile took the monkey back. The monkey jumped on the tree and never spoke to the crocodile again.

Friendship is all about trust.

23 The Silver Key

A traveller decided to spend the night at a guest house. He knocked at the door of the only guest house in town. The owner of the guest house was a very greedy man. When he realised that a customer was knocking at the door, he said, "Dear sir, welcome to the guest house. Sadly, I have lost the key. The door will open only when you use a silver key."

The traveller understood at once, that the owner was hinting at a silver coin. But there was no other guest house in town, so he decided to put in a silver coin through the keyhole. The owner promptly opened the door.

When the owner was showing the house to the traveller, the smart traveller locked the owner in the storeroom and exclaimed, "Oh! I am so sorry. I am unable to find the key. I guess this door, too, shall open with a silver key."

The greedy owner had to put a silver coin through the keyhole. Only then did the traveller let him out.

As you sow, so you reap.

24 The Dishonest Doctor

A blind old woman called a doctor to cure her. The doctor told her that the treatment would be expensive. The old woman agreed, but put forth a condition that if the treatment didn't work, she wouldn't pay him a single penny.

The doctor started coming to her house to give her the treatment every day. As the lady was blind, the dishonest doctor decided to take advantage of her. He stole her expensive china, carpets, silk bedsheets and furniture.

When the old woman got her eyesight back, her house was bare. She looked around and said to the doctor, "I won't pay you a penny!"

"But ma'am," the doctor said, "your eyesight is cured. And as per your promise, you should pay my fees."

To this, the woman replied, "Well, I do not think my eyesight has been cured completely. And that's because I can't see any furniture, bedsheets or china in my house!"

If you try to outsmart others, they may also outsmart you.

25 The Rotten Apple

A boy fell into bad company. His father was worried. He decided to give his son some advice. He showed the boy a basket full of rotten apples. He asked the boy to put a healthy, red apple in the basket. The boy did as he was asked.

The next day, the father showed the basket to his son. They saw that the healthy apple had also turned rotten. The father explained, "That is why company matters. You must be careful of who you choose to be with."

Be wise in choosing your friends.

26 Patient Little Girl

A village was struck by a great famine. Everyone was starving. The king decided to distribute a basket full of bread among the villagers. On seeing the food, the villagers started fighting. But there was one little girl, who waited patiently for her turn.

She got a last, little piece of bread. When she began eating the bread, she found a silver coin in it. The honest girl took it to the king. The king was so impressed by the girl's honesty that he let her keep the coin and also gave her enough food to last a while.

Honesty is thet best policy.

27 The Blind Man's Lamp

A blind man moved around with a lamp at night. Everyone wondered how the lamp helped this blind man. But no one asked him. One day, a curious boy asked the blind man, "Why do you carry a lamp around? You can't even see!"

"I don't carry the lamp for myself, boy!" the blind man replied. "I carry it so that people like you, who can see, don't bump into a blind man like me."

There is always a reason behind every action.

28 The Lazy King

A king had lots of money. He didn't need to do anything. So he simply lazed around. He didn't eat nutritious food and he didn't exercise. One day, he fell ill. He just couldn't move.

All the wealth that he had was now useless. That was when his advisor said, "Sire, if you do not take care of your health, you will not be able to enjoy your wealth."

Health is wealth.

29 The Monkey Weighs the Cake

Two cats got into a fight over a piece of cake. They both fought so loudly that a monkey, who was passing by, decided to intervene.

"Hey, kitties," the monkey said. "Why are you fighting so loudly over a piece of cake?"

One cat replied, "We both saw it. And now she won't let me eat it!"

"Ah!" the monkey exclaimed, "that's not fair. Give me the cake and I will cut it into two equal pieces. Then you both won't have anything to fight over."

The cats gave the piece of cake to the monkey. He brought out a weighing scale, cut the cake into two and put a piece on each side of the weighing scale. One piece weighed more. So, the monkey ate a part of the heavier piece. Now the other piece weighed more. The monkey ate a part of the other piece.

Finally, two tiny pieces of the cake were left. The cats now realised their folly. They were about to take the two tiny pieces when the monkey put the remaining cake in his mouth.

"That was my commission for solving your quarrel," he said.

Beware of those who take advantage of other people's quarrels.

30 Half the Profit

An apple seller wanted to sell juicy, delicious apples to the king. He filled a basket with the apples and set out for the palace. He was stopped by the gatekeeper.

"What are you carrying in the basket?" asked the gatekeeper.

"I want to sell these delicious apples to the king," the apple seller said.

The gatekeeper replied, "You can go in. But there's a condition. Promise to give me half of whatever profit you earn."

The apple seller didn't like the gatekeeper taking advantage of his position. But he agreed. He went in and gave the basket of apples to the king. The king loved the apples and offered to pay the apple seller fifty gold coins. But the apple seller replied, "Oh no, your Majesty. Pease give me the reward of ten whip lashes. And give five of them to your gatekeeper, as he wanted to share my profit."

Cheating people will only bring trouble.

31 The Slave and the Lion

A slave in the king's palace always dreamed of running away. One night, he found a chance and ran into the jungle. There he met a lion. The lion would have attacked the slave. But he was in pain. A nail was stuck in his paw.

The lion held up his injured paw and asked the slave for help. The slave readily helped the lion. The lion was grateful and they soon became friends.

Some days later, the slave was caught. The king was furious at the slave for running away. He asked his soldiers to put the slave into a lion's cage, so that the lion would eat him up.

When the slave entered the lion's cage, he realised that it was the same lion he had helped. The lion, too, recognised the slave and refused to eat him.

The king was impressed with this friendship. He set the slave and the lion free.

If you help others, others will help you.

1 The Magic Pot and the Greedy King

A farmer was tilling his field. Suddenly, his axe hit a pot and got stuck to it. The farmer looked at the pot and found nothing unusual. He let the axe remain in the pot and went to eat lunch. When he returned, he found five axes in the pot. It was a magic pot! Whatever you put in it, would multiply.

The farmer added grains and money, and grew rich in no time. He decided to take this pot to the king. The farmer thought that the king would be very happy with this gift and would reward him.

The king was indeed very happy. He gave the farmer a few gold coins and kept the pot. First, the king put a little gold into the pot. The gold multiplied. Then, he put in his finest dresses. They multiplied, too. The king's happiness knew no bounds.

He was so happy that he started dancing around the pot. Suddenly, his foot slipped and he fell into the pot. Out came five new kings. All the kings started fighting with each other for the throne. The five kings killed each other in the end.

Greed always leads to problems.

187

② The Monkey and the Jar

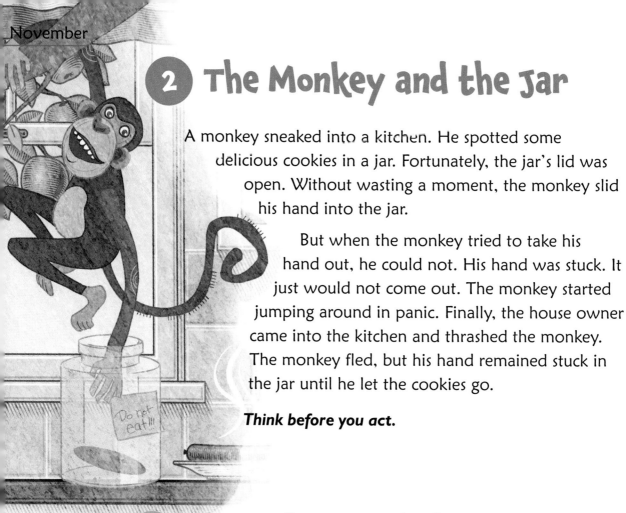

A monkey sneaked into a kitchen. He spotted some delicious cookies in a jar. Fortunately, the jar's lid was open. Without wasting a moment, the monkey slid his hand into the jar.

But when the monkey tried to take his hand out, he could not. His hand was stuck. It just would not come out. The monkey started jumping around in panic. Finally, the house owner came into the kitchen and thrashed the monkey. The monkey fled, but his hand remained stuck in the jar until he let the cookies go.

Think before you act.

③ The Palace and the Hut

A king decided to build a beautiful palace on top of a mountain. When the construction of the palace was complete, the king went to inspect it. He saw an ugly hut near the palace.

"What is this hut doing near my palace?" the king asked the engineer.

"Your Majesty, an old lady lives there. She says this hut is very dear to her. We tried offering her money, but she would not let us demolish the hut," the engineer said.

"Let it be there," the king said, "it will remind me that there are certain things money can't buy."

Everything can't be bought by money.

4 The Pigeon Among Crows

A farmer was fed up of the crows near his farm. Every time he grew a crop, the crows would destroy it. Nothing he did would scare them away.

The annoyed farmer put up a scarecrow to shoo the crows away. But the crows pulled it down and destroyed the scarecrow. The farmer was worried. Then he had an idea. He spread a big net across the field.

Far away, the crows were preparing to raid the field and eat the juicy corns. They were talking very excitedly when a pigeon approached them. "May I also eat the corns with you?" asked the pigeon.

"Why not?" said the crows and invited the pigeon to raid the field.

Just when the crows and the pigeon landed on the field, the net caught them and trapped them all. When the farmer came to kill the crows, he spotted the pigeon among them.

"You chose the wrong company, dear pigeon," the farmer said. "Now I will have to get rid of you, too."

One has to pay the price of choosing the wrong company.

5 The Robin and the Crows

A robin was flying in the sky. Suddenly, a bunch of crows started teasing her and called her names. The robin ignored them, flew away and settled cosily in the hollow of a tree.

Soon it started raining heavily. The crows didn't have any shelter. They saw from afar that the robin was nice and dry in the tree's hollow.

"Will she let us in?" one crow asked, "we teased her so much!"

The crows finally asked the robin. She generously let them in and saved them from the rains. The crows never teased the robin again.

Do not carry grudges.

6 The Cruel Hunter and the Rabbit

A cruel hunter once caught a rabbit. The rabbit begged and pleaded for mercy. The hunter laughed wickedly and said, "I am going to cut your throat and roast you over the fire! I am going to eat you!"

Just as the hunter was about to kill the rabbit, there was terrible thunder and lightning. The knife slipped from his hand and fell on his foot. The sharp knife cut the hunter's foot and the rabbit slipped away from his hands. The rabbit quickly escaped.

If you are cruel to others, you too will be in pain.

7 The Trees and the Lions

This is the story of two trees who lived in a forest. They were very happy. But there was one problem. They didn't like the oh-so-many animals that kept running all around the forest. The lions were the worst. They would roar loudly all the time, which annoyed the trees a lot.

The two trees thought of a plan. They would shake violently whenever an animal came near them. Slowly, the animals of the jungle assumed that something was wrong with the jungle. They started leaving it. The lions too, left and settled in another jungle. The two trees were finally at peace.

The ferocious lions of the jungle had kept the humans from cutting down the forest to build cities. When the humans found out that the lions had left the jungle, they came with their axes and chopped down all the trees.

That was the end of the two trees and all the peace that they wanted.

If you upset nature's balance, you will have to pay for it.

191

8 The Cruel Lion and the Man

Once a man caught and trapped a lion. He spent many years in a cage. One day, a kind man was passing by. The lion asked the man, "Could you please let me out? I am hungry and weak."

The man looked at the lion and said, "If I let you out, you will eat me."

"No, my friend," the lion said. "How could I eat the one who set me free?"

The man trusted the lion and opened the latch of the cage. The lion came out and said, "I am very hungry. Sorry friend, but I will have to eat you."

The man was aghast. He saw a fox walking by, so he asked the fox for help.The lion growled, "This man is my food. I have all the right to eat it!"

"Oh! yes, you do," the fox said, "but could you show me how it happened?"

The lion, with the idea of explaining to the fox, went inside the cage. As soon as he was inside, the fox latched the cage and said to the man, "Don't trust your predators."

Do not trust your enemies.

9 The Foolish Lion and the Smart Deer

A deer was grazing in a forest with her fawns. Suddenly she saw a lion approaching. She took her fawns inside the lion's den. From there, she started speaking loudly in a weird voice. "Look children, here comes the lion. Today we will eat him for our dinner. His flesh is really delicious."

On hearing this, the lion got scared. He started moving away from his den when he bumped into a jackal. "Why are you not going inside your den?" the jackal asked.

"There's a strange animal in my den who wants to eat me," the lion said.

"There's no one more powerful than you in this jungle," the jackal said, "let's take a look at who is in the den."

The lion looked doubtful. He said to the jackal, "I know you will leave me and run away." On hearing this, the jackal tied his tail to the lion's and assured him that he wouldn't run away.

When the deer saw them approaching, she said, "Oh look! The jackal has captured the lion and is bringing him here." On hearing this, the lion fled, dragging the jackal with him.

You can face any difficulty if you are smart.

10 The Starfish on the Beach

A huge storm hit the sea. Many starfish got swept onto the beach. They were dying on the sand when a boy started picking them up and throwing them back into the sea.

Looking at the boy's efforts, a man said, "There are thousands of starfish lying here. It's not going to make much of a difference to anyone."

The boy looked at the man and then at the starfish in his hand. He said, "It will make a difference to this starfish."

Don't hesitate to make a difference, however small it might be.

11 The Sleepy Teacher

A teacher in a school often slept during his class. One day, a student mustered the courage to ask the teacher, "Why do you sleep during the lecture?"

The teacher said, "I sleep because I need to meet the great sages in my dream."

One day, a few students fell asleep during the teacher's lecture. The teacher woke them up and asked, "Why are you sleeping?"

"We went to meet the sages too," the students said, "We enquired about you. But they said they didn't know anyone by your name."

You get what you give.

12 The End of the Vase

A Zen monk broke his master's favourite vase. The monk was very scared. He hid the broken vase and waited for his teacher to return. When his master returned, the monk asked, "Why is death necessary?"

The master explained, "It is a cycle. Everything that lives has to die. It is the rule."

On hearing this, the monk said, "The time had come for your vase to die, master."

The master smiled and forgave his disciple.

Difficult situations should be handled with tact.

13 The Jar of Sweets

Danny loved to eat sweets. His mother would worry that if she left him alone at home, he would eat all the sweets in the house, and fall sick.

One day, mother had to go out. As soon as she left, Danny got hold of the jar of sweets and slid his hand inside. He grabbed a fistful of sweets, but his hand would not come out. When mother came back and saw Danny's plight, she said, "I kept the sweets in a jar with a narrow mouth. You can only take one sweet at a time."

Sometimes we get stuck because of greed.

14 The Catapult

A naughty boy enjoyed hitting people with stones from his catapult. Once a bald man was walking under the tree on which the boy was sitting. The boy aimed and hit the bald man's head.

The bald man's head started bleeding. But instead of scolding the boy, he told him, "Your aim is very good. Tomorrow, the king will pass by this very road. You should hit him too on his head. He will be impressed and reward you handsomely."

The boy liked the idea. The next day, he waited for the king.

The king's procession passed under the tree. The boy aimed at the king's head and hit him. The king's head also started bleeding. However, instead of rewarding him, the king asked his guards to fetch the naughty boy.

The boy was punished severely. He promised never to hurt anyone for fun.

Naughty actions meet bad ends.

15 The Sneaky Monk

John was a monk who lived in a monastery. He had the habit of jumping the monastery wall and going out every night after everyone was asleep. No one knew about this habit.

One night, John checked to see if his master was asleep. He then tiptoed, adjusted the ladder and climbed out of the monastery boundary. He had a long, leisurely walk.

But that night, John's master was not asleep. He had seen John peeping into his room and followed him. He saw John climb over a ladder and cross the monastery's boundary wall that night.

The master removed the ladder and waited for John to return. When John came back, the master helped him climb down the wall. On seeing his master, John got scared. He thought that he would get punished.

But master only said, "Don't forget to take your shawl, John. It's cold at night."

Seeing his master's love, John gave up his habit of going out stealthily.

Love can reform anyone.

16 The Coward Who Joined the Army

A coward lived in a quaint little village. He would be scared of the slightest of noise. At night, even if the crickets made a sound, the man would hide under the bed.

One day, a king's messenger came to the village. He announced that a war had broken out and the king needed all the young men to work as soldiers.

The coward loved the king. He too joined the army. He wore the soldier's uniform. He was given the job of patrolling the jungle and checking that no enemy sneaked in through the jungle. But at night the coward was very frightened.

He could barely walk. Whenever he heard the crows on the tree or the leaves rustling, he would stop hide behind a bush. As a result, he could not keep an eye on the enemy and three spies sneaked into the kingdom.

The king got killed the next day and the coward went back to his village, feeling very guilty and ashamed.

Always perform a job that suits your capabilities.

17 The Goat and the Donkey

A trader owned a donkey and a goat. The donkey would carry the load all day. He worked without complaining. The goat didn't have anything to do as the trader needed her only for her milk.

So the goat felt ignored and jealous.

One evening, as the donkey was resting, the goat went to him and said, "You work so hard all day. I bet you need a vacation. Tomorrow, when master calls you, pretend to be ill and refuse to work. You will get some rest."

The innocent donkey agreed. He did as the goat said. The master took him to the doctor. The doctor examined the donkey and said, "Your donkey has a strange health problem. He needs to drink the soup made from a goat's heart to get well."

Without thinking, the master killed the goat and prepared soup for the donkey.

Jealousy will always meet a sad end.

18 The Smart Donkey

A trader loved his donkey very much. One day, he left his donkey to graze in the public lawn. The king's guards arrived and started shooing the donkey away. When the trader saw this, he yelled at the guards, "What do you think you are doing?"

The guards replied, "We are shooing this good-for-nothing animal away."

"Don't you dare call my donkey that," the trader cried, "he is much better than the king's ministers."

When the king heard the trader's words, he was furious. He called for the trader and asked, "I heard that you called my ministers more worthless than a donkey?"

"I made no mistake, your Majesty," the trader said. "Once, while crossing the bridge, my donkey's foot got stuck in a gap. Since then, he is always careful while crossing the bridge. But even after so many losses, your ministers continue to empty the royal treasury."

The king understood what the trader was hinting at. He pulled up all his ministers and reprimanded them for their dishonesty.

A wise person always learns from his mistakes.

19 The Shipwreck

There was a small village by the sea. Once a ship got wrecked near the shore because of the captain's carelessness. All the people in the ship drowned. One villager felt really sad on seeing such a disaster.

He said, "God is so unjust. So many people had to lose their lives just because of one person. That was really unfair."

While the man was commenting on God's ways, a red ant bit him on his ankle. When the man looked down, he saw that many red ants had surrounded his feet. He began stamping on the ants and killed many ants.

A voice of God said, "One ant bit you and you've killed so many. And you comment on my unjust ways. Shouldn't you look at your actions first?"

Look at yourself before accusing others.

20 The Cat Who Changed Into a Girl

A cat was strolling in a garden. She came across a handsome boy and instantly fell in love with him. She wanted to marry him. But a cat cannot possibly marry a human. So the cat prayed hard. Finally, God asked her, "What do you want, dear cat?"

"I have fallen in love with a boy," the cat said. "Please turn me into a girl. I want to marry him."

God realised that the cat was indeed in love. He turned her into a girl. The cat went to the boy, who also fell in love with her.

Finally, the day of their marriage arrived. The boy and the cat-girl were saying their vows when God decided to test the cat-girl. He sent a mouse scampering into the church.

The cat-girl's senses grew alert. When she saw the mouse, she forgot all about the wedding vows and started chasing it. She didn't stop until she had caught the mouse.

God was aghast. He had changed the cat's body, but he couldn't change the cat's mind. He turned her back to her original cat self.

You can change appearances, but you can't change character so easily.

21 The Bandit's Stick

A man was moving through a dark jungle when a robber attacked him. The robber looted the man of his money and his donkey. When the robber was leaving, the man stopped him. "Excuse me," he said. "Will you give me your stick?"

The puzzled robber asked, "Why do you want my stick?" The man replied without hesitation, "You see, I need to give my wife something when I return home. You have taken everything else. At least give me the stick."

When the robber gave the man his stick, the man thrashed the robber and shooed him away.

Sharp and quick thinking helps you in troubled times.

22 The King and the Magic Dumbbells

Once there was a lazy king. He wouldn't exercise at all. This made him fall ill. The royal doctor was called. He gave the king a pair of dumbbells and said, "Your Majesty, these are magic dumbbells. If you swing them for an hour every day, you will always be healthy and happy."

The king followed the doctor's advice, not realising that he was exercising daily. He grew fit and healthy. He called for the doctor and said, "These are indeed magic dumbbells!"

The doctor replied, "If you keep using them, you will remain healthy. If you stop, you will fall ill."

If you can't convince someone in one way, try another.

23 The Witty Boy and the Shopkeeper

A woman sent her witty son to buy half a kilogram of apples. When the shopkeeper saw that he was just a small boy, he decided to cheat him. Instead of half a kilogram, the shopkeeper gave the boy apples much less in weight.

But the boy was smart. He realised that the shopkeeper was cheating him and not giving him all the apples. He asked the man, "These apple don't look like they weigh half a kilogram. Why aren't you giving me all the apples?"

The shopkeeper replied, "Oh don't worry. These weigh half a kilogram. Anyway, carrying less will be easier for a small boy like you."

When the shopkeeper asked for money, the boy paid him less.

"Why are you paying me less?" the shopkeeper asked.

"Don't worry," the witty boy said. "Less money will be easier for you to count."

The shopkeeper looked sheepish and gave the boy the right number of apples. He was always careful of the witty boy in the future.

Wit solves many problems.

24 The Old Man and the Young Man

An old man and a young man met on the road. They started talking. The young man was going to meet his beautiful girlfriend. The old man was going to a religious gathering.

The young man said to the old man, "Come with me and meet my beautiful girl. You will be happy to see her."

The old man declined the offer and said, "You should come to the religious gathering with me. It cleanses the soul." The young man was excited to see his girlfriend, so he politely refused.

After some time, both men parted ways. But they couldn't stop thinking about each other. The old man wondered if he had done something wrong by missing an opportunity to meet a beautiful girl. The young man kept wondering if he had missed an opportunity to cleanse his soul.

This way, both men remained distracted throughout the evening.

Do not get swayed by the choices others make.

25 The Priest and the Boatman

A miserly priest lived in a village. He hated spending money on anything. The villagers knew about this quality and most of them stayed away from him.

Once the priest had to cross a river. He got into a boat and asked the boatman to row. The boatman quoted his fee for the service. The priest just smiled. When the boat started moving, the priest said to the boatman, "What will you do with the money? I will give you the treasure of knowledge." He started reciting all the religious tales he knew.

The boatman soon got tired of listening to the priest. He knew that this was the priest's way of avoiding the fee. When the boat reached the middle of the river, the boatman started rocking it violently. The priest went crashing into the river!

"Help! Help!" the priest shouted, "I don't know how to swim!"

"You know so many other things," the boatman said. "Wouldn't all that save you?"

After a while, the boatman took pity on the priest and pulled him up. The priest had learnt his lesson.

Don't try to weasel out of paying your dues.

26 The Frog Who Lied

There was once a frog who claimed that the lake he lived in had magical powers. He told all the animals in the forest that if they drank water from the lake, they would grow strong.

A monkey on the tree finally grew fed up and said. "If the water in your lake is really magical, why are your legs so weak? Why are you still hopping from one place to another?"

Everyone started laughing at the lying frog.

Think before you speak.

27 A Job for Everyone

A lion was assigning jobs to all the animals in the jungle. Finally, only the hare, tortoise and donkey remained. A monkey chuckled and said, "The hare is a timid animal, the tortoise moves far too slowly and the donkey is just plain dumb. What job will you give them, Oh King?"

The lion thought for a moment and said, "Don't laugh, foolish monkey. The hare runs fast and could be a messenger. The tortoise could lie still as a rock and be a spy and the donkey is strong enough to carry my belongings when I travel."

Each one has his own worth.

28 Following Instincts

There lived a young boy in a village. His name was David. He was very determined. One day, he went to his friend's house. His friend asked, "Why are you here?"

David replied, "Yesterday, I thought that if your land is tilled, many beautiful plants would grow in it."

The friend laughed loudly at David. "I think that your courtyard has a lot of gold hidden under it. You could dig it and see if my instinct comes true."

David agreed, He reached his courtyard and started tilling his land. After a few hours, his plough hit a metallic object. When David examined closely, he found that there was indeed gold buried under his field. He had struck a pot full of gold!

David suddenly became a rich man. And that was only because he had the faith and determination to follow his instinct. David didn't have to worry about money for the rest of his life.

Always have the courage to follow your instinct.

29 The Hermit and the Old Woman

A hermit lived in a village. He made a living by collecting alms from everyone. In the same village lived a miserly old lady. One day, the hermit knocked on the old lady's door and asked for alms. The old lady reluctantly gave him last night's leftovers. The next day, the hermit knocked on her door again. The old lady was very angry.

She mixed some poison in the rice. But soon realised that this was a mean thing to do. She gave him fresh rice instead. The hermit gladly took the rice and left. On his way, he found a hungry man and gave away his rice. The man ate the rice and blessed the hermit. He was the old woman's son. When he told his mother about the rice the hermit gave him, the old woman thanked god that she had decided not to be evil.

If you wish ill for others, ill will come upon you.

30 The Clever Wife and the Grinding Stone

A farmer's wife was unhappy because her husband would invite his friends for dinner every night. One day, the farmer invited his friends and went out to get some milk. When his friends entered the house, they saw a grinding stone decorated with a garland.

"What's that?" they asked. "That's my husband's God," the wife said. "He hits the guests with it every day as a ritual." The guests fled. When the farmer returned, he asked his wife. "Why did the guests run away?"

"They asked for your favourite grinding stone," the wife said. "But I refused to give it to them. So they went away."

Every problem can be solved with a little wisdom.

1 The Brave Boy

A poor boy was travelling through a jungle. A group of robbers surrounded him and asked him for money. The boy said, "I won't give you anything. You may do what you want."

The robbers caught hold of him. The boy started struggling and fighting. But he was not strong enough for all the robbers, who soon overpowered him. When they checked the boy's pockets, all they got was a single coin.

The leader of the robbers said, "He is indeed a brave boy, who fought so much for one coin. Let him go."

Bravery will always be rewarded.

2 The Fishermen and the Treasure

A fisherman led his group of friends to catch fish in the sea. The group kept throwing their net in the sea from morning to evening, but were unable to catch anything valuable. The leader refused to give up.

In the evening, when they threw the net, the remains of a shipwreck got caught in the net. The fishermen pulled the net up and saw that a box full of treasures had got entangled in the net.

The fishermen were rich!

Hard work gives good rewards.

3 Lost and Found and Lost Again

There was a boy who bought a candle for four pence. He went home and lit the candle. Just then, a coin fell from his hand in the dark. The boy used the candle to look for the coin and kept looking.

Finally, when the candle was almost burnt out, the boy found the coin, which was worth just one pence. But the candle worth four pence was over. The boy didn't know whether he had found money or lost it.

We keep looking for little things and lose out on bigger ones.

4 The Lucky Gardener

A gardener in a kingdom would choose the choicest of fruits and bring them on a platter for the king every day. One day, the gardener chose some cherries for the king.

The king was in a foul mood that day. When he ate the cherries, he found them to be sour. He threw the cherries at the gardener. "Thank God for showing mercy!" the gardener said.

The king asked, "Why are you thanking God when I just insulted you?"

The gardener said, "I was about to get pineapples for you, Your Majesty."

Always look at the bright side.

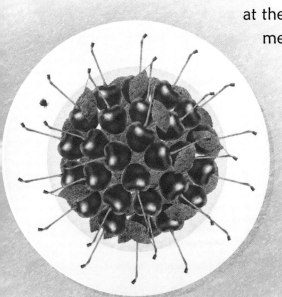

5 The Shining Roofs

A man was lazing on his verandah when he spotted the glittering roof of a house in the valley.

"There's a house of gold," he yelled and ran down into the valley. Once there, he saw that the house was just ordinary.

When he looked up, he saw that the roof of his house was glittering. He ran all the way to his house when he realised that the pieces of broken glass he had kept on the roof were reflecting the sunlight. The man had learnt a valuable lesson.

All that glitters is not gold.

6 Green Gold

A little girl made a living by begging. One day, a lady gave her a handful of seeds and said, "Sow them and take care of them. You will become rich."

The girl sowed the seeds. They grew into beautiful plants with pretty flowers. She went from door to door selling the flowers and earned money. Soon, she set up her own little flower shop.

The little girl never begged again.

Plants are precious.

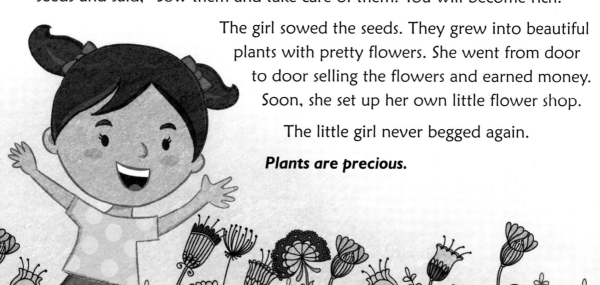

7 The Cat Becomes a Pet

Long ago, a cat lived in the wild. It wanted to stay with the strongest animal. So, it walked with the lion. But the lion ran away when the elephant came, so the cat started walking with the elephant.

One day, they met a hunter. The elephant ran away. So the cat went home with the hunter. On seeing the cat, the hunter's wife yelled, "What will I do with this cat?"

Just then, a rat scampered into the house. The cat ran after the rat and caught it. The hunter's wife let the cat stay in the house.

Change is the only constant in nature.

8 The Robber's fate

A man robbed a businessman and beat him up badly. When the businessman's family screamed for help, the robber ran away. He got chased by a fox, so he climbed a tree. On that tree lived a cobra, who came out and was about to strike the man with its fangs. The man jumped into the river.

In that river was a crocodile who ate him up. When the businessman's family came to know about it, they felt happy at nature's justice.

Nature always does justice.

9 The Farmer's Concern

During a war, a king camped near a village. He told his soldiers to get vegetables from the nearby field. The soldiers went to a large field. A farmer was standing there. The soldiers asked the farmer, "It is the king's order to bring vegetables. Can we take vegetables from this field?"

The farmer took them to a smaller field, "That field was not mine, so I couldn't grant you permission. This is my field. Take whatever you want."

The king rewarded the farmer for his concern.

Have concern for others' property.

10 The Camel Who Teased Everybody

A camel had a nasty habit of teasing everybody. He would laugh at the speed of the tortoise, the long ears of the hare, the lion's mane and the horse's tail.

One day, a monkey, who was fed up with the camel's behaviour, asked the camel, "Why do you walk around with that ugly hump? Don't you ever brush your teeth? They are so yellow! And look at your long, ugly neck. Ugh!"

That day, the camel realised his mistake and stopped teasing everyone.

Nobody is perfect.

11 The Parrot and the Dog

A parrot lived with a family in the city. In the same house lived a dog. Every day, the dog would see the parrot enjoy a meal of spicy, green chillies.

One day, the dog was tempted. He asked the parrot, "Are the chillies tasty?"

The parrot replied, "They are delicious!"

The dog put a big chilli in his mouth. But it was so spicy that it burnt his mouth. The dog regretted listening to the parrot.

One man's delicacy is another man's poison.

12 The Shark's Teeth

A shark was very proud of his teeth. He would snap his teeth and scare anyone who crossed his path. All the fish were scared of the shark. They decided to teach him a lesson.

They said to the shark, "If your teeth are so strong, why don't you bite into a rock?"

The foolish shark said, "Why not?" and bit into a rock. All his sharp teeth fell off.

Pride comes to a fall.

13 Snake in the Carriage

A man who wanted to travel by train reached the station at the last moment. All the carriages were crowded. He went to a shop nearby and bought a rubber snake. He threw it in the crowded carriage. Everyone instantly emptied it. The man happily settled in a seat.

After some time, he realised that the carriage hadn't moved. He asked the station master, "Why isn't the train departing?"

"Oh, the train has already left," the station master said. "There's a snake in this carriage, so it was separated from the train.

Being oversmart lands you in trouble.

14 The King and the Pond

A king wanted to appoint a patient man as his minister. He called all the contenders and gave each of them a bucket with a hole. He asked them to empty a pond with the bucket.

One by one, the contenders started giving up. There was only one man left. He continued filling the bucket and throwing the water out. Finally, the pond was empty. The man found a diamond ring at the bottom. He gave it to the king.

"That's your reward, my man," said the king and appointed him.

Patience is a virtue.

15 Four Blind Bandits

A man was going through a dark jungle at night. Suddenly, four bandits surrounded him and took away all his money. They were about to kill him when the man said, "You can't kill me. An astrologer has said that only four blindfolded men will be able to kill me."

The dacoits blindfolded themselves in order to kill the man. The man took advantage of the moment and ran away.

Quick wit is always an advantage.

16 The Proud Hermit

A hermit meditated for many years. God was happy with him and granted him superhuman powers. The humble hermit soon grew very proud of his powers. He would show them off whenever he got a chance.

One day, the hermit had to cross a river. Instead of taking a ferry, he used his superpower and walked across the river. He was smiling smugly, when a sage sitting nearby said, "You fool, you could have paid ten coins instead of wasting your superpower on this!"

The hermit was ashamed.

Pride makes us do foolish things.

217

17 The Potter's Pots

A potter made earthen pots. Such pots are fragile and break very easily. His customers often complained about this. The potter grew tired of their complaints and prayed to God, "Please make my pots unbreakable."

God granted his wish. The pots wouldn't break. Sadly, this stopped his customers from returning to buy new pots. The potter started losing money. He prayed again, "Please make my pots the way they used to be."

God smiled and did the needful.

Be happy with what you have.

18 The Mango Tree and Banyan Tree

A mango tree and a banyan tree lived in the garden. Everyone loved to eat the fruits of the mango tree and it was usually surrounded by people. This made the mango tree proud. It said to the banyan tree, "Everyone loves me, but no one cares for you."

One day, the king's guards came into the garden. They wanted mangoes. They plucked the mangoes roughly out of the tree and even broke some of its branches. The bruised mango tree realised its mistake.

Pride can cause a great fall.

19 The Fox Who Ate a Pumpkin

A fox ventured into a garden where many pumpkins grew. He was hungry, so he ate a pumpkin. Just then, the gardener came and saw what the fox had done. The fox pleaded for mercy but the gardener set his tail on fire.

The fox was angry. He ran into a field of wheat. This field belonged to the same gardener. The fox set the entire field on fire with his burning tail. The gardener repented his actions.

It's better to forgive small mistakes.

20 The King's Treasurer

The king's treasurer had grown old, so he resigned from the job. The king needed a new treasurer. He called all the young men who wished to apply for the post.

He filled their pockets with gold coins and asked them to dance. The condition was for them to dance until the king asked them to stop. As soon as the young men started dancing, gold coins fell out of their pockets. All but one man stopped to pick up the coins.

The king looked at the man and said, "This man will be my treasurer."

Don't let money distract you from doing your job.

21 The Merchant in the Sinking Boat

A rich merchant was travelling by boat. Suddenly, there was a storm and the boat started sinking. While everyone jumped off the boat or held on to floating logs, the merchant stayed on and prayed.

A wise man advised him, "Don't pray, just jump and save yourself." But the merchant didn't pay heed. Everyone was saved, but the merchant drowned with the boat.

God helps those who help themselves.

22 The Snake and the Frogs

Once, two groups of frogs in a well got into a fight. They fought bitterly for many days. One group went to the snake and told him about the situation. They requested the snake to eat the rival group.

The snake started living in the well. He would eat three frogs of the rival group every day. Soon, all the frogs of the rival group were eaten. The frogs requested the snake to leave. But the snake refused to do so and also ate up the frogs who had asked for help.

Do not ask for help from your enemy.

23 The Donkey and the Lion

The lion invited all the animals for his birthday party. All the animals had a gala time, but the donkey didn't turn up. The next day, when the lion saw the donkey, he asked, "Why didn't you come to the party?"

The donkey said, "I don't like parties. I decided to stay at home."

The donkey spoke the truth, but the way in which he said it offended the lion. The lion was angry and he threw the donkey out of the jungle.

Bitter truth should always be told tactfully.

24 The Miser and the Coconut Tree

There lived a miser in a city. One day, he went to buy a coconut. "Ten rupees," the coconut seller said. "I will only give you five," the miser said. "Go to the village. You will get the coconut for five," the coconut seller said.

The miser walked to the village and said, "I will buy the coconut for three rupees." A villager pointed the miser to a tree and said, "Climb the tree and get your coconut for free.

When the miser climbed, he slipped and fell. He had to pay a thousand rupees for the treatment.

Sometimes, to save a little money, we end up spending more.

25 The Monkey in the Zoo

A monkey went from town to town, showing off his antics with his master. He worked very hard, but got little to eat. One day, he saw a monkey in the zoo and noticed people giving him lots of food.

The monkey ran away from his master and joined the zoo. For some days, he was happy with the free food. But he started getting bored. There was nothing to do! He ran back to his master, who welcomed him warmly.

Hard work is better than sitting idle.

26 The Cat and the Chickens

Some chickens fell ill in a coop. A cat, who wanted to eat the chickens for some time now, thought that he finally got a good chance. He dressed up as a doctor and tried to get into the coop.

"I have come to treat the chickens," the cat said, "let me in, please."

But the chickens were smart. They said, "We are feeling much better now. We don't need a doctor. Thank you."

And that is how the chickens got saved from the cat's claws.

Wisdom helps us sail tough times.

27 The Class Monitor

A teacher took her class for a picnic. Louis was appointed as the monitor. The teacher told Louis, "It's your duty to see that no one puts their hands or heads out of the bus windows." Louis took charge and watched over the boys carefully.

When everyone was getting back into the bus, the teacher caught Louis putting his head out. "You are such an irresponsible monitor," she yelled.

"Ma'am, I was just checking to see if everyone got in," Louis explained. The teacher felt ashamed for shouting at poor Louis.

Think before you speak.

28 The Court Jester

The king had a jester who was very funny and witty. The only problem was that he usually made the king the butt of his jokes. One day, the king was furious and ordered the jester to be hanged.

When the jester was brought to be hanged, the king asked, "What's your last wish?"

The jester smiled and said, "To die of old age."

The king laughed at his witty reply and set him free.

Wit saves us in tricky situations.

29 The Thief and the Merchant

Two men were put together in a lodge. One of them was a rich merchant and the other was a thief. When the thief found out that the merchant had a big diamond, he decided to steal it.

The thief searched all the merchant's belongings when the latter was sleeping, but found nothing. The next morning, the thief told the merchant, "I am a thief and I searched everywhere, but I couldn't find your diamond."

"That's because I hid the diamond in your bag," the clever merchant said. "I knew you wouldn't check there."

Clever thinking helps us save ourselves from dishonest people.

30 The Bull and the Mouse

One day, a mouse was feeling very bouncy and happy. He just couldn't sit still, so he kept running up and down. He came across a sleeping bull and disturbed its sleep.

The furious bull started chasing the mouse. But the mouse was quick and nimble on his feet, so he ran fast and hid into his hole. The bull ran after him, but crashed into the wall and got hurt.

The bull learnt an important lesson that day.

A small creature might not always be weak.

31 Telling the Truth

A rich man had a heart problem. The doctor advised his servant to keep the rich man away from any shocking news that could give him a heart attack.

One day, the rich man went on a long vacation. In his absence, some unfortunate events took place.

Upon the master's return, the servant said, "The mice are running everywhere in the house."

The rich man asked, "Why isn't the cat hunting them down?"

The servant replied, "The cat didn't get any milk, so it ran away."

The rich man said, "Didn't the cook give the cat any milk?"

The servant replied, "The cook didn't get his wages, so he didn't turn up."

The rich man asked, "Didn't my wife give him any wages?"

The servant said, "Your wife has been asleep since you left for your vacation."

The rich man asked, "Has she become that lazy?"

The servant said, "There was an accident. Your wife broke her leg while cleaning the house. The doctor has advised her bed rest."

This way, the servant delivered alarming news without shocking his master.

Bitter truth should be told gently.

OTHER TITLES IN THIS SERIES

ISBN 978-93-83202-81-2

ISBN 978-93-84625-92-4

ISBN 978-81-87107-53-8

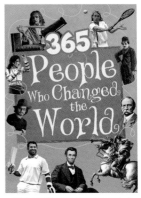
ISBN 978-93-84225-34-6

ISBN 978-93-80070-79-7

ISBN 978-93-80069-35-7

ISBN 978-93-80069-36-4

ISBN 978-93-81607-49-7

ISBN 978-93-84225-32-2

ISBN 978-81-87107-52-1

ISBN 978-93-84225-33-9

ISBN 978-93-80070-83-4

ISBN 978-93-80070-84-1

ISBN 978-81-87107-55-2

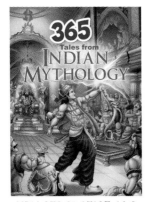
ISBN 978-81-87107-46-0

ISBN 978-81-87107-58-3

ISBN 978-81-87107-56-9

ISBN 978-81-87107-57-6